Children of RaShell

jodi jensen

Contents

To my son, Joshua, who sparked an idea in me without even knowing it. This story would not exist without you.

One

Xander opened his eyes to pitch blackness and the sound of children's laughter. The joyful noise filled the air, resonating deep in his soul, while the urge to seek the source overwhelmed him. But as the cobwebs cleared from his mind, his muscles tensed.

Something was wrong.

Everything was wrong.

He searched his brain for the answer to the *wrongness* around him.

Then it hit him.

Bloody fucking hell.

There were no children left. Not for almost twenty years now.

He scrambled to his feet, fumbling through the darkness, moving toward the sound. His hands scraped along a cold, jagged rock wall and he tripped over the uneven ground. A wave of nausea washed over him, and his stomach churned as goosebumps raced down his arms.

Still, he persevered, winding his way through tunnel after tunnel, the continual childish giggles in the distance his only guide.

At last, the deep, dark, utter blackness lifted a fraction, enough that he saw shadows and shades of gray. He knew he was getting closer.

Occasional words echoed through the air now, hanging as if trapped within the stone walls alongside him.

"…free!"

The peals of laughter were louder with every step, the shadows lightening.

Up ahead, he saw a tiny figure crouched in the crook of the tunnel, just out of sight from the other direction.

A child. It has to be.

But hiding from who? Or what? His body tensed as his gaze darted around, searching for the threat.

"Neriah, you can come out now. Felicity called *olly olly oxen free!*"

The girl stood, but stayed hidden, scrawny

shoulders shaking with suppressed laughter.

Xander frowned, the feeling of wrongness stronger than ever.

There're no children left, and sure as hell no games or laughing…those are nothing but remnants of a world long gone…

Stepping lightly, he moved closer to the kid. So close he could smell the *cleanness* radiating from the tattered clothing. He wrinkled his nose at the scent. It'd been years since he'd smelled anything so fresh, and the incongruity of it made him uneasy.

"Aria says she won't play anymore if you don't come out!" the same voice shouted.

Xander froze. He hadn't noticed the first time, but that voice was feminine—and naggingly familiar. He'd heard it before.

Everything seemed to spin around him, and he slapped his hand against the cold rock wall to steady himself.

The child turned at the noise, then backed right into the wall she'd been hiding behind, eyes wide.

Maybe I'm hallucinating…

He reached for the girl, desperate to find out if she was real.

The child launched herself away from the wall and ran.

Still staggering, Xander had a flash from his own

childhood. Teacups tilted at crazy angles and spinning as shrieks of delight blended with carnival music in the background. That's what he felt like now—a dizzy, nauseous, and overwhelmed kid doing that drunken stumble after riding the teacups.

"Wait—" he croaked.

But the girl had disappeared.

Bile crept up into his throat and he swallowed hard, over and over, trying to keep his stomach in check. He turned a corner and discovered a muted glow ahead.

A few more steps and he found himself in an enormous cavern with an underground lake in the center. Shafts of light streamed down from a series of cracks in the rock ceiling, illuminating the crystal-clear water. The shores surrounding the lake were littered with rough shelters, campfires, and people.

Legs wobbling and hands trembling, he glanced around, looking for the source of the laughter that'd drawn him here.

There...

His gaze came to rest on a brown-skinned woman with a white-haired girl clinging to her side.

Alarm bells went off in his head. He knew her.

Sabine—

The woman's name flashed in his mind. How or where he knew her from, he didn't know. The only thing he knew with any certainty was that she shouldn't be here.

Another child peeked out from behind her, then a third poked her head out from a crude shelter nearby.

Xander's stomach lurched at the sight of the three albino girls. He staggered back, sagging against the rock wall as his knees buckled.

They shouldn't be here either.

None of them should.

Two

"Water, Aria, hurry!" Sabine ordered as she rushed to Xander's side. She bit her bottom lip as her hands patted his arms, legs, and torso, looking for injuries and finding none. "Are you okay? Where the hell've you been?"

His brow wrinkled as his dark brown eyes clouded with confusion. "You know me?"

"Xander." She cupped his cheek. "It's me, Sabine. Of course, I know you."

His face paled, and he jerked his head to the side to puke in the dirt.

She scrambled back, her thoughts churning a mile a minute. She hadn't been sick like this when she'd arrived. He was three days late getting here, though, which meant a greater chance he was exposed to the toxic air on the surface.

"Here." Aria, the eldest of the children, seven in human years, but fourteen in clone years, thrust a water pouch in Sabine's direction. The girl's eyes never left Xander. "What's the matter with him?"

"Toxin poisoning," Sabine explained. She gave Aria what she hoped was an encouraging smile. "The water will help him. It just takes a little while. Now, take your sisters and go get today's rations."

"Felicity, Neriah, c'mon! We're going to The Square!" Aria scurried away, sisters in tow.

Xander tried to sit up as the girls left, one hand on his aching head.

"Let's get you comfortable," Sabine said, helping him scoot back until he was propped against the tire of an old truck bed. Patting his shoulder, she peered at him. "Better?"

He nodded, though the confusion hadn't left his eyes as he looked around.

"What do you remember?"

He frowned. "Where am I? What is this place?"

"Drink," she said, handing him the water pouch.

After several sips, he asked again, "Where am I?"

"Fertile Lake." She glanced at the nearby shore where a water wheel was turning. "You don't remember anything?"

"You said you're Sabine." He held up his hand to stop her before she could do more than nod. "I remember that now, but I don't recall where I know you from."

"What else?"

"Those kids…" His frown deepened. "They're not—they shouldn't be here."

"Have some more water," she urged, motioning to the pouch. "It'll come to you. And check your pockets for me. You should have some samples on you somewhere."

"Samples?" He glanced down at his brown jacket, plain black t-shirt, and cargo pants. "Samples of what?" he asked as he thrust his hands into various pockets, pulling out his used mask, an empty food pouch, and a nametag with *X. Mitchell* on it. Finally, from an inside zippered pocket of his jacket, he produced a small bag.

She took the bag and set it on the ground next to her, deciding to wait until she got him settled before looking through it. "Do you think you can stand?"

Xander shook his head, turned his face to the side, and retched again. His body trembled, beads of sweat breaking out on his forehead.

"Sit tight, I'll be right back. And keep sipping that water." Hurrying in the same direction the girls had gone, she stopped at the first shelter she came to. Made with scavenged lumber from long abandoned homes on the surface and a thatch roof, the hut served only to

17

provide a bit of privacy. She poked her head through the open door and peered into the dim recesses. "Dalton?"

"Back here," he called.

Sabine went inside. "I need your help."

An older man with a wild muss of wiry gray hair and a scruffy beard came out of the only other room in the dwelling. "What's up?"

"Xander finally made it, but he's sick. I need to get him to my infirmary." She headed out the door, glancing back to be sure Dalton was following.

"Did he bring the samples?"

"He did, but I'll have to look at them later. He's in pretty rough shape." As they got closer to where she'd left him, her heart skipped a beat. Xander was slumped over to the side, unconscious again. She rushed to him, dropping to her knees in the dirt. "Xander? Hey." She gave him a gentle shake. "Wake up."

Dalton stopped by Xander's feet. "Let's lay him down."

Together, they moved him, and Sabine pressed an ear to his chest. "He's breathing, heartbeat sounds strong. He's burning up, though."

"You want to take him to my place for now?" Dalton offered. "It's closer."

"Yeah, we better do that, thanks," she said, glancing at the detached truck bed trailer she'd leaned him against. It made a good cart. "I know it's not far, but I'd

18

rather not drag him. Let's use this."

Dalton grabbed Xander under the arms while Sabine took his feet and they lifted him into the cart.

"Good thing this is empty," she remarked. "He takes up the whole bed."

"I haven't picked up today's vegetables yet." Dalton nodded at the pen off to the side of his shelter. "I'll fetch the ponies."

"And I'll find the girls. They should've been back by now." Sabine surveyed the distance between Dalton's place and the village center, known simply as 'The Square'. It wasn't too far, only a few minutes' walk. Plenty of time had passed for the girls to have returned.

Dalton patted her shoulder. "Don't worry, I'm sure they're fine. Probably got distracted playing."

"How'd you know that's what I was thinking?"

"You're staring at The Square with your face all screwed up in that worried look." At her frown, Dalton grinned. "Yep, that's the one right there."

She went and picked up the bag of samples, then forced a fake smile. "Back in a few."

"You're not fooling anyone," Dalton called after her.

"Not trying to," she hollered over her shoulder. She stowed the samples in the small backpack she always wore as she hustled down the well-used trail. The dirt was hard-packed from years of use, and wide enough for two carts to pass each other.

A few minutes later, Sabine reached the outer edge of The Square. While the rest of the cavern had a perpetual muted glow from the beams of light shining down on the lake, combined with warm blooms of constantly burning campfires, The Square was lit with torches, candles, and a bonfire in the center.

She paused next to a booth offering meat pies, her mouth watering at the scent. Not only was there no time for such a treat, but she had nothing on her to barter with. Life in the cavern was a series of trades—even the daily rations for herself and the girls were a result of her contributions to the community.

Scanning the collection of booths, she spotted a familiar mop of white hair among a crowd gathered near the fabric booth and headed that way. Angry words and curses rose amidst the people, and as she got closer, she heard a child crying.

"Aria!" she called, pushing through the crowd.

At the sound of her name, Aria turned and met Sabine's gaze, waving frantically.

Sabine went around the last clump of people to find Neriah, the youngest of the girls, held in the booth owner's grip. Iver wasn't known for his calm demeanor. She hurried forward, snatched the crying child from him, and gathered the girl into her arms. "What's the meaning of this?"

"She took a piece of ribbon. Now she needs to be punished." Iver scowled at Neriah, thrusting his hand out to show a length of blue ribbon clutched in his fist as evidence.

"All she did was touch it," Aria protested.

"It's ruined—see?" Iver opened his fist. The ribbon lay limp and grubby across his palm. "It's nothing but rubbish now. I can't trade it, can't even give it to my wife to use!"

Sabine glanced at the ribbon, then at a nearby woman in the crowd, whose own yellow ribbon was in far worse shape than the blue one. Neriah sobbed against her shoulder. Sighing, Sabine patted the child's back and nodded at Iver. "I'll bring you payment later. I've got something to take care of first."

"That 'something' better be punishing the little thief!" His face flushed, and he spat into the dirt at her feet.

Sabine's arms tightened around Neriah. "Now you listen here," she raised her voice as her own anger rose. "I'll take care of her how I see fit. These girls are my responsibility and I said I'd bring payment later. What I do with her is none of your concern." She turned to Aria, who was clutching Felicity's hand, both girls staring wide-eyed at the scene. "Did you get the rations?"

Aria gave a solemn nod, then looked at her sister.

"In her bag."

Felicity gripped the bag lying crossways over her shoulder. "Can we go now?" she whispered, tears welling in her eyes.

Shifting Neriah to her hip, Sabine held out a hand to Felicity, who clasped it in a death grip. "Yes, let's get out of here."

As she walked away with the three girls in tow, she had to remind herself most of these people had been down here for years, some more than a decade. They hadn't been told the girls were second generation clones, or that their developmental rate, both physically and mentally, was double that of a human. The three-year-old clinging to her was, in reality, a six-year-old, though smaller in stature than the average human equivalent.

The only thing most of these people knew was Sabine worked on the surface at RaShell Bionics' medical facility, had escaped, and came down here to join their colony with three orphaned children. She used her medical experience to trade for food, water, and shelter, which gave her access to the limited medical equipment available, including a crude microscope. Only Dalton knew the truth about her and RaShell—she needed an ally, after all. And a place to continue her research and experiments.

With Xander's arrival, and the samples, she hoped to prove her theory about the lake was correct.

Sabine picked up the pace as they left The Square behind them. "Let's hurry, girls. Xander needs our help."

Three

Is that...humming?

Xander turned over, bunching the blanket over his throbbing head. He couldn't remember what the hell he'd done last night, but this hangover had to be the worst he'd ever had.

Clanging and cursing from the other room filtered through the threadbare quilt and he heaved a long-suffering sigh and sat up. It only took a second to realize there was a problem.

This wasn't his room.

He squinted into the murkiness, the familiarity of that act jogging his memory. Tunnels...darkness...moving figures among the shadows...a kid...

Sabine! And the girls—

He jumped off the cot, his head screaming at the abrupt movement. Pausing to take a few deep breaths, he covered his eyes to block the dim light coming from the open doorway.

The humming continued, interspersed with—was that a *neigh*?

What the hell was going on? And where the hell was he?

Removing his hand slowly from his face, he blinked until the double vision improved before making his way into the next room.

An older man, with bushy gray hair sticking up every which way and a moth-eaten beard, glanced up from chopping vegetables and grinned. "You're awake! Sabine will be pleased."

"You know—" The words came out hoarse and gravelly. Xander cleared his throat, then tried again. "You know Sabine?"

"Sure do!" The man tossed a handful of wilted carrot tops into a bin with some other scraps and reached for a turnip. "Do you remember who you are?"

"Xander Mitchell," he said with a frown. "And you are…?"

"Dalton, friend of Sabine's." He motioned to a small table in the corner, then went to a cupboard and withdrew a tin cup. "Take a seat and I'll get you some

26

coffee—it's chicory root, so don't get too excited. Sabine ought to be back any minute now."

Xander sat and watched as Dalton stirred a pot of the hot drink on the woodstove, his mind racing the whole time. Bits of his memory were returning: Sabine asking for his help, a nursery full of albino babies, RaShell's first pregnant clone—*oh shit! R1*—he needed to get the news to Sabine. Fighting against the sudden wave of nausea, he moved to stand. "I need to see her right away, if you'll just point me—"

"Woah, woah, woah there." Dalton dropped the tin cup with a clatter and rushed over, easing Xander back into his chair. "You don't look so hot. Whatever it is can wait until she gets here—"

"I'm here," Sabine said, ducking into the room. Her expression brightened at the sight of Xander. "You're up, good. How do you feel?"

"Never mind that." His gaze flickered to the trio of white-haired girls with her. "We need to talk, privately."

Dalton retrieved the tin cup and filled it with the steaming hot chicory coffee. He set it in front of Xander, then picked up the pail with the vegetable scraps in it and looked at the girls. "C'mon you lot, let's get the ponies back to their stall and fed." He handed the bucket to the middle girl, then took the smallest one by the hand as they left.

"What's wrong?" Sabine asked, the instant they

27

were gone.

"R1—she gave birth—"

"Already? That's sooner than expected. I mean, of course, everything about them is accelerated, but—"

"She didn't survive," he said bluntly. "Neither did the baby."

"Damn," she whispered, shaking her head. "What happened? Tell me what you know."

Xander took a sip from his cup as she spoke, but when the coffee scalded his tongue, he set it back down to cool further. "It's not much. All I know is what they tell us during daily security briefings. They said she'd given birth to a fully developed child, but neither of them lived."

Sabine clasped her hands on the tabletop, and her brow furrowed. "Fully developed, my ass. The pregnancy was too quick. We engineered the fetuses to reach full term in six months. Even with the genetic modifications, a child can't develop in less than four months."

"That's all I know. I couldn't stick around to see if there were rumors of anything different. I had to leave on schedule." It was all coming back to him as he talked with her. The shock and sorrow at the facility over the loss of R1 and her baby, the fifteen-minute window for him to sneak away that Sabine had arranged for him, collecting the samples—the samples... "I had some trouble getting into the greenhouses. I got everything you asked for, but it wasn't easy. They have more guards there than before. I guess some topsiders have been breaking in and stealing food."

"Can you blame them?" she huffed. "People are starving up there, dying of toxin poisoning from drinking unsafe water. I can fix this, I know I can. I just have to—"

"How sure are you, though?" He picked up his cup again and blew across the surface before taking another sip—just right—not coffee exactly, but similar enough and rich tasting with a woody, but nutty, flavor.

"You're proof, if I needed any," she said, smiling at him. "You had toxin poisoning when you got here. I gave you some water from Fertile Lake, and now look at you. Almost right as rain."

He raised an eyebrow. "Almost?"

"Don't worry, you'll make a full recovery, likely by the time you've finished that coffee." She stood and faced the tiny room. "What did you ingest, anyway? It would help my data to know what made you sick."

"My food and water were both from RaShell. I only ate and drank half rations for a few days prior, stocking up for the journey here." He thought for a moment, recalling a brief period when he'd been in the greenhouse and a guard did an unexpected walk-through. "It must've been the air."

"You weren't using your mask on the surface?" Her eyes widened, and she clucked her tongue in disapproval. "Why on earth not?"

"I had to get out of the greenhouse quickly, so I wasn't seen. No time to put it on until I was already outside."

"Damn, it really only takes a few breaths. Further proof, as if I needed any." She glanced at the doorway as Dalton and the girls approached, their laughter and happy chatter filling the air. "We need to get these samples back to my place for testing. Are you feeling up for a walk?"

Xander downed the rest of his chicory coffee in four steaming gulps, then nodded. "Ready when you are."

ك ك ك

"You girls like it down here?" Xander asked, as they set out.

Felicity held his hand and grinned up at him. "Oh yes! We get to help Dalton feed his ponies and rabbits, and Sabine lets us play games, too. We never got to do that before."

"Yeah, up top we always had to study and be studied," Aria chipped in. She tucked a strand of white hair behind her delicate pale pink ear. "We help Sabine a little, but she's nice to us, so we don't mind."

Sabine picked up Neriah, who kept stopping to

fetch rocks in the path, and settled the girl on her hip. "We try to have fun, don't we?" She glanced at Xander. "I know you'll want to see The Square, but I think we'll save that for another day. We had an issue earlier."

"Issue?" He frowned, his gaze going to the busy street market ahead. "What kind of issue?"

Pointing to a path that deviated around The Square, Sabine filled him in as they walked.

When she was done, Neriah laid her head on Sabine's shoulder. "I never seen such a pretty blue."

"You just need to look in the mirror, sweetie," Sabine said. "You and your sisters have the same pretty blue eyes."

"Prettier than the ribbon?" Neriah asked, perking up.

"Much prettier than the ribbon. They're the color of the crystal blue water in the lake," Sabine assured the little girl.

Felicity squeezed Xander's hand. "She just wanted to touch it. She wasn't going to steal it. That man was mean."

"Yes, he was being mean," Sabine agreed. "I'll take his payment to him later and it'll be fine."

"Do you ever get used to the dark down here? It feels like dusk that lasts forever." Xander's gaze roamed his surroundings, the rocky walls and ceiling, the series of trails winding all over, everything muted shades of brown and gray, and at the center of it all, the lake. With the light streaming from above the water, and compared to everything else, it almost seemed as if it was glowing.

"What's dusk?" Felicity asked, her eyes wide and curious.

"When I was a boy, the skies on the surface were often blue with puffy clouds and the sun shining bright yellow. Dusk is that time of day right after sunset. Not light anymore, but not quite dark, either. Dim and dusky, like now." The memory of those long gone beautiful blue skies made him look to Sabine with renewed determination. "You really think we can fix things?"

"I do." She smiled, setting Neriah down and taking a firm hold of her hand. "Why else would we be here?"

Satisfied, Xander turned back to Felicity, then glanced at Aria. "Maybe you'll see a blue sky one day."

Aria nodded and skipped ahead a few paces. "That would be lovely!"

He chuckled at the display of exuberance, not something he was used to seeing. His job at RaShell had been all about keeping the building secure. He had nothing to do with the children or their care. He only knew Sabine because they worked the same shift and frequented the employee cafeteria at the same time. After weeks of mutually shared friendly smiles and greetings, he'd struck up a conversation. They'd become fast friends and had been ever since.

They made small talk for the rest of the walk, careful not to say too much about their plans in front of the children.

Finally, Sabine pointed to a smaller trail that veered off the main one. "That's my place over there."

Xander followed her to a group of shelters situated in a semi-circle around a firepit with the cavern wall behind.

"We sleep here," Sabine said, nodding at the closest structure. "The one in the middle is the infirmary. I stay close in case I have a patient to check on during the night, but that's rare, so far at least. The last one is my lab."

His gaze traveled over the three lean-tos: rugged looking, but practical. All of them had three sides and pitched roofs, with the front open to the fire. A couple of blankets were hanging inside their living space and infirmary, giving what he supposed was a tiny bit of privacy.

"There's no power down here, so we're rudimentary at best, but we make it work. Hardest part is the lab. I'm restricted to what I can see with my microscope." She set Neriah down and gently patted her on the back. "Go on and play, but stay close. Aria, look after your sisters, please."

As the girls ran off, Sabine turned to Xander. "How are you feeling? Do you need to rest? More water?

Food?"

"I'm fine," he said, realizing that he really *was* fine. His nausea was gone, same with the headache and other symptoms. And his memory had returned. "You were right about the lake water. I feel amazing."

Sabine's shoulders relaxed, the relief on her face noticeable. "I want to get started with these samples—"

"After you," he said, motioning to the lab.

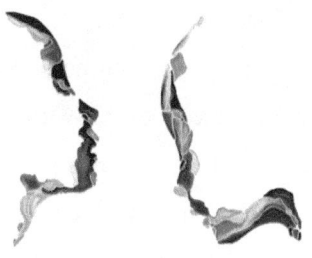

Four

Sabine lit the oil lamps in her lab, then took the samples from her backpack. Inside the zippered bag were a bunch of smaller bags. Some had water, the labels identifying the different sources, while several more had soil. There were half a dozen plant species, and three animal: an earthworm, a beetle, and a tiny frog with four eyes instead of two. A small metal case revealed vials of blood—taken from RaShell's lab, she presumed—clamped into place and surrounded with packing material. Lastly, there were three bags with empty vials sealed inside. The labels on those read: *RaShell Bionics*, *Surface*, and *Cave*.

She glanced at Xander, who was studying her microscope. "Are these air samples?"

"They are," he confirmed.

She nodded, her mind immediately going to work on solving the problem of how to test them. In the meantime, she had plenty of others to work with. "Here, help me sort the soil samples, we'll start with those."

They put them in order of geographical location, beginning with the one taken from the greenhouse, then along the route to the cavern.

"I want to get these onto slides, two for each sample. After that, we'll treat one with water from Fertile Lake, and leave the other untreated." She glanced up and motioned to a nearby basin. "Wash up before we start. Once these are all prepped, we'll go get a few more soil samples from here. I've looked at the soil before, of course, but I want fresh samples for comparison."

"That'll give me a chance to see more of the lake anyway," he said, as he stood and went to scrub his hands.

"I haven't even been all the way around it myself," she admitted. "Dalton tells me it stretches for miles and there are people living clear at the other end."

He looked at her with a raised eyebrow. "You haven't been tempted to explore?"

"Of course, but I haven't had time. Things work on a barter and trade system here. In order to keep myself and the girls fed, I've had to trade what limited medical skills I have, which means I need to be available here."

She flashed him a quick glance from where she was lining up the slides on a wooden tabletop. "Not that they usually need much in the way of healing, not with the lake and its water accessible to all."

"Does the lake water cure everything?"

"That's what I'm trying to find out," she said with a smile. "But I think so, yes. From everything I've seen, the air is pure here, as is the soil. And on the rare occasion I'm needed, it's for a smashed finger, or a cut, things like that. You're the first sick person I've treated, and all I did was give you water from the lake."

"Incredible."

The awe in his hushed voice made her look up again. "It really is, isn't it? This could change everything on the surface, if I'm right." She touched one of the bagged samples. "I'm hoping we're about to take the first step in restoring the world above."

"Go big or go home, right?" He grinned as he joined her at the table. "What can I do to help?"

Handing him a pair of tweezers, she waved a hand at the small pile. "You load the dirt. I'll add the water?"

"Sounds good to me."

A half-hour later, the first set of experiments were laid out and initial data recorded. All they could do now was wait for the water to work its magic.

Sabine stored the other samples in a wood box, then slid it under the table. Reaching for her backpack, she said, "I think it's past time I slip away to do some exploring. Let's get the girls and take that walk, shall we?"

"You got anything to eat before we go?" Xander looked hopefully around the lab.

"Well, not in here." She chuckled as she led him out of the lab, across the campsite, and into her living quarters. Rifling through the single cupboard near the washbasin, she produced a heel of bread, the last of yesterday's rations. "This is about the only thing I've got that's portable. There's hardtack, but it needs to be soaked before it's edible. We'll do that tonight with our supper."

Accepting the bread, he bit off a chunk and nodded.

She handed him her canteen, which she always kept full. "Let's bring this too."

"After you," he said, around a mouthful of food.

Stepping out of her lean-to, she saw the girls nearby, drawing in the dirt with sticks. "You three ready for a walk?"

Aria was the first to look up, a smile spreading across her face. "Where are we going?"

"Exploring!" Sabine watched as they abandoned their game. "What were you playing?" she asked as they joined her and Xander.

"Tic-tac-toe!" Felicity exclaimed. "I was winning!"

"Ah, yes, you're so good at that one!" Sabine turned to Xander. "They excel at strategy and problem-solving. It's part of their second-generation programming. This game's a bit too easy for them, but they play mostly so Neriah can play too. I think they secretly enjoy it."

He leaned in close, his voice low in her ear. "They know they're clones?"

She chuckled, eyeing the girls, who all had excellent hearing. "They do know, though Neriah," she reached down and tousled the child's hair, "doesn't understand as much about what that means as her sisters do."

Xander gave a thoughtful nod, his shoulders relaxing. "I probably know less than anyone here, about programming anyway."

"Maybe," she shrugged, then motioned to the path leading away from the campsite, "but you know plenty I don't know about RaShell's security protocols. That'll come in handy, I'm sure."

The path came to a fork a short distance later, one side swerving back toward The Square, the other side going in the opposite direction. Taking the second option, they headed away from the hub of the settlement. It wasn't long before the trail narrowed, snaking between boulder sized rocks, the lake only visible in glimpses as they passed. Soon after, the ceiling sloped, and they stood at the opening of a tunnel.

"Are you sure we're going the right way?" Aria looked back and forth between Sabine and Xander, her gaze settling on Sabine.

"Well, I haven't seen any other trails, so we must be." Sabine took a box of matches and two small lanterns from her pack, then lit them. "We never go anywhere without the lanterns," she said to Xander, handing him one. "Get too far from the lake or a campsite, and it's really dark."

He held the lantern up to the entrance and peered inside. "Any dangerous animals to watch for?"

"We see snakes sometimes," Felicity said, slipping her hand into Xander's.

"Plus, frogs, rats, and lizards, things like that," Aria added.

"Nothing to be scared of, right?" Sabine grasped Neriah's hand and smiled.

"Right!" the three girls chorused.

Laughing, Xander shook his head as he entered the tunnel with Felicity in tow.

Aria went next, and Sabine brought up the rear with Neriah.

"It's a bit cooler in here, isn't it girls?" Sabine asked. "Can anyone tell me why that is?"

"Well, I know that caves stay almost the same temperature all the time because they're not affected by the weather," Aria said. "But tunnels don't get as much air circulating or moving. Could that be why?"

"That's part of it," Sabine agreed. "Felicity? Any ideas?"

"The absence of light!" Felicity let go of Xander's hand and twirled once. "Over by the lake there's light coming in from above, but none here," she said with a curtsey.

Sabine couldn't help but giggle at Felicity's cute display. "That's right. Natural light helps to keep the cave warmer, but the tunnels don't have any. Hey, while we're here, let's grab a sample." She handed her lantern to Aria and removed her backpack. After scooping up a portion of dirt and filling the baggie, she marked the sample, and they resumed their journey.

The tunnel twisted through the bowels of the cave, water seeping down the side walls in places, taking them further and further underground. Finally, ahead, was a dim glow.

"There must be people," Xander said, picking up the pace.

"Must be one of the deeper settlements Dalton told me about." Sabine doused her lantern once it was light enough to see without it. "Fuel is hard to come by," she said, when Xander gave her a curious look. "We only use these when we have to."

Nodding, he followed suit, extinguishing the tiny

flame.

Without the lanterns, the tunnel threw long shadows along the ground and walls, but the light ahead continued to grow brighter as they moved toward it. A few voices echoed in the air, bouncing off the rock walls around them.

"I don't like that sound," Neriah said, frowning up at Sabine.

Giving her hand a squeeze, Sabine smiled. "It's just people, honey. It only sounds funny because we're in the tunnel. It'll all be back to normal once we're out, you'll see."

"Depends on what you consider normal," Xander said, coming to a halt at the mouth of the cavern.

The hairs on her neck rose at his tone. "What is it?" she asked, as she came up behind him.

"See for yourself."

She moved into the opening and her jaw dropped. "Oh…"

Before them, at least half a dozen pregnant women and even more children milled about the small settlement.

Five

Xander stood in shock, staring, convinced he couldn't really be seeing what he was seeing. There hadn't been any pregnant women in years, and the only children he'd seen were the albino girls from RaShell.

Yet, here they were, boys and girls with varying shades of hair color and skin tones, ranging from an infant carried in a sling to a boy who looked to be about the same age as Aria.

Incredible!

But how did this happen?

He glanced at Sabine to find her grinning from ear to ear.

"My God," she said in a hushed whisper. "You

know what this means?" She didn't wait for an answer. "Genetic engineering might not be necessary anymore. I mean, we still have to prove it's due to the healing properties of the lake water, but..." she turned to Xander, her eyes lit with excitement, "it's the lake, it has to be."

His own excitement was building as well. "How? How do we prove that?"

"Let's go talk to them," she suggested.

"Sabine?" Aria spoke up, her voice uncertain. "This means you don't need us anymore?"

"Oh, sweetie, no, it doesn't mean that at all." Sabine put her arm around Aria's shoulders. "We still need you and your sisters. Your lives matter. We just hope it means—well," her gaze flickered to Xander, then back, "it might mean you girls don't need to worry about having babies."

Xander's pulse spiked at her words. If that were true, RaShell could stop wasting time and resources trying to preserve humans and worry about fixing the planet, healing the surface of the disease left from the toxins. People could reproduce naturally.

"Can we play with them?" Felicity asked, hopeful.

"Let's go find out," Sabine said, stepping from the shadows of the tunnel.

Xander's hand went automatically to his hip, where he usually carried his weapon, but nothing was there.

He'd left it behind because of the tracker in it. While it was true there didn't appear to be a threat, the thought of confronting the unknown without protection still left him unsettled.

Positioning himself in front of the girls, he stayed by Sabine's side as she approached a group of four women in varying stages of pregnancy and a handful of toddlers playing nearby.

"Hello!" Sabine said brightly.

Three of the women scurried away, gathering the toddlers with hushed whispers, and disappearing into a hut.

"It's okay." Sabine held out her hands in supplication. "We're from the settlement across the lake."

The remaining woman, a tall brunette with an enormous belly, eyed them suspiciously. "I lived there until I got pregnant and had to move here for my own safety, and I've never seen you before." Her gaze flickered to the girls, who were peeking out from behind Xander. "Haven't seen them either, and I think I'd remember if I had."

Xander held his tongue, deciding it was better to let Sabine handle the situation, as she was the one who'd been living down here. Glancing covertly around the small community, he saw huts, campfires, woven baskets, and crude toys scattered everywhere. He didn't see any men, only women and children. He forced himself to relax his hands as well as his posture, there was no threat here.

"My name is Sabine, this is Xander, and the girls are Aria, Felicity, and Neriah," she said, stepping aside to gesture at each of them in turn. "What's your name?"

"Marina," the woman said, studying Xander's clothes. "You're from up there, aren't you?"

Xander gave a nod and a cautious smile, unsure of how he'd be received. "That obvious?"

"No one down here wears anything like that." Marina glanced at the girls, then Sabine. "Albinos?"

Sabine tucked Neriah up against her side and nodded.

"You're all from up there," Marina concluded, her gaze narrowing. "What do you want?"

"To help," Sabine replied. "Would it be okay if Xander took the girls to play while we talk?" She gave him a hopeful glance, and he shrugged. "They'll stay in sight while we speak uninterrupted."

After a slight hesitation, Marina gestured to a rag ball lying on the ground nearby. "Belongs to my son. He won't mind."

Xander and Aria looked at each other, and he smiled at the girl. "Go get it. I'll show you how to play kickball." He took the girls to a small open space where he could still see Sabine, but couldn't hear what she and

Marina were saying.

"What's kickball?" Aria asked, tossing the ball from one hand to the other.

"Easy..." Xander looked around, and spotting a few rocks lying about, moved them so he had two on one side of the clearing, spaced roughly ten feet apart, and two on the other end placed the same.

"Neriah will be on my team, and we'll try to kick the ball between those two rocks. Aria and Felicity, you'll be the other team and you try to kick the ball to the rocks on the other side. You can't use your hands, only your feet."

With that, he put the ball on the ground and pointed to Felicity. "You kick first."

It took a few tries, but before long the girls had the hang of the game and all three of them were running circles around him. Soon, the other children from the settlement wandered over, watching from the sidelines, grinning and pointing. A couple of them even cheered when Aria made a goal.

"Hey, can we play?" a young boy piped up.

Xander glanced over to where Sabine and Marina were still deep in conversation, then motioned to the boy to join them. "Anyone else?"

Four other children stepped forward and Xander decided to watch from the sidelines while the kids played. It didn't take long until the clearing was filled with laughing, panting, grunting, and cheering.

Soon after, Sabine and Marina joined him.

"Looks like fun," Marina remarked, seeming much more at ease now.

"I used to play when I was a boy." Xander gave her a small smile at the memory, then turned to Sabine.

The look on her face could only be described as ecstatic. "There are twenty-three children here and nine pregnant women…can you believe that?"

Stunned by the news, his own grin widened. "That's amazing!"

"And that's not all, Xander, there's another settlement like this one on the other side of the lake!"

His gaze flashed to Marina. "Really?"

She nodded, her own eyes bright with excitement. "We divided between two camps because we were outgrowing this one. I haven't been over there," she said, rubbing her swollen belly, "but last I heard, they've got nearly double the expectant mothers and while the children are younger, there are more of them."

"You had no idea?" he asked Sabine.

She shook her head. "I get it, though. They're protecting these women and children. I've seen young adults in The Square, but I didn't realize most of them were born and raised here."

"Incredible…" He glanced at Marina with a newfound level of respect.

"I know!" Sabine enthused. "They've been having children all along down here. All of their younger population is from natural reproduction." She kept one eye on the kickball game in progress, the other divided between Marina and Xander. "This is the most fantastic news. Do you realize what this means?"

While he had an idea, he couldn't have understood the scope, not the way she did as a geneticist. And he didn't know how much she was going to tell Marina. He waited for her to elaborate.

"I need to go up top, back to RaShell. I need to talk to Gavin."

"Right now?" Xander asked, startled.

Sabine smiled. "Tomorrow, or maybe the next day. There's work to do first."

Six

ours had passed before Sabine, Xander, and the girls got back to camp. With no natural light to tell time by, the days tended to go by in a blur, the weeks running together. They ate when hungry, slept when tired, and life developed its own natural rhythm.

"Aria, can you get the hardtack soaking for me, please? And throw a couple pieces of wood on that fire." At the girl's nod, Sabine turned to Xander. "Let's go look at our soil samples. We'll need to compare them to the soil we gathered from our trek. Those are probably the healthiest samples we're going to find."

Glancing at Aria, Xander frowned. "Should she be messing with the fire?"

Sabine smiled. "Though she's only seven years old, her internal development and cognizant skills are fourteen. Double time internal growth, remember?"

"Ah, that's right." With a final peep over his shoulder at the oldest of the girls, Xander fell in step with Sabine.

"The microscope is already put together, so I'll view the slides if you'll record the data for me." Without waiting for an answer, she entered the lab, lit her oil lamps, then took the logbook off the shelf. She retrieved the microscope from its cupboard and set about organizing the samples. Looking up, she found him standing there, awaiting instructions. "Take a seat." She motioned to the end of the table where there was a clear spot for the book, a pen, and a stool.

"The tab marked 'soil' I presume?" he asked, opening the log.

"You got it." Picking up the first of a pair of slides, she said aloud, "Greenhouse, untreated." Bending, she scooted a light close to her, positioned her slide under the lens, then peered through the eyepiece. "No visible microorganisms or organic matter. Soil volume is less than, say, ten percent." She paused to glance at Xander. "Ideally, it should be fifty percent, but this is a bit of guesswork, as I have no way of accurately measuring the volume."

Xander nodded as he wrote. "Got it. Anything

else?"

"There's little to no water that I can see, appears dry and more like dirt than soil." She removed the slide, then picked up the next one. "Greenhouse, treated." Her heart skipped a beat. "There's a diverse number of microorganisms and organic matter, species not discernable with this microscope, as they're too blurry to make out in detail, but I can see they're there. Soil volume appears to be close to the ideal fifty percent ratio, while the soil itself is rich in color and moist, indicating a good balance of water."

"That's amazing," Xander said, still scribbling furiously in the logbook. "All that happened to the greenhouse soil in the time we were gone?"

"It did." She grinned, excitement coursing through her. "Imagine what this means for the surface. Healthy, restored soil means crops, trees, and all sorts of vegetation can thrive again. And all without any type of genetic modification!"

"That would be incredible! The world could reset."

She examined the rest of the soil samples he'd brought, along with the ones collected in the cave and tunnel. The data stayed true to the patterns she'd seen thus far. Once the last of the data was recorded, she sat back on her stool, eyeing Xander.

The look of awe on his face further bolstered her determination. "Help me clear these slides and we'll get some new ones set up for the plants. I want to see what happens to the surface specimens you brought when treated with the lake water."

"Are you saving the soil samples?"

"I wish I could, but I've no way to store them. We've got the data, though, and if necessary, I can replicate the comparisons for Gavin. I only used a fraction of the collected soil." She piled the soil into a tiny heap on the table, handing each slide to Xander to wipe clean. Once they finished, they laid out the plant samples and treated half of them. "Much as I'd like to sit here and watch the process under the microscope, I'd better go check on the girls and get some food going for our supper. You coming?"

"Of course." Standing, he brushed his hands off and fell in step beside her.

"Hope you're not expecting anything fancy," she said with a smile. "Aside from fish, fresh meat is pretty scarce, unless you like rat. The few livestock they've got are used for milk and cheese. Plenty of vegetables, though."

"I'll take fish over rat any day, though protein is protein."

"Most of the produce is root vegetables. Those are more efficient to grow. They take up less space in the fields near the lake and the yield is higher. Potatoes, carrots, onions, turnips, all the makings of a hearty stew.

How's that sound?"

"Like it'll take a while to cook," he said, his voice ringing with disappointment.

"Nah, we pretty much always keep a pot of water simmering. I have some fish stock in the kettle right now, so I'll just toss in some veggies and by the time the hardtack is soft, it'll be ready."

Xander's stomach gave a loud grumble. "Er…sounds good to me."

Chuckling, Sabine glanced over to where the girls were playing hopscotch. "I taught them that one. Had to find games they could play while I worked and with nothing but sticks and rocks, we've had to be inventive."

"They're amazing—much cleverer than I'd realized." He motioned to the fire. "Aria did a good job of stoking this thing."

"She did even better than that—look." Sabine pointed to a stump where a pile of chopped vegetables lay. "They must be hungry, too."

"So, they *do* eat?"

She looked at him, surprised. "Of course. Why wouldn't they?"

Xander shrugged. "I don't know. You know I don't know much about them. My job was security, so I rarely saw them."

"True, still…" She nudged his shoulder. "How do you feel about gutting a couple of fish for me?"

"Lead the way," he said with a grin.

A little while later, full on vegetable stew and fish, Sabine sat watching Xander and the girls playing dots and boxes in the dirt. Seemed like they were all getting on well, which she was grateful for. It'd be one less thing to worry about when she left for the surface.

After tossing another log onto the fire, she went and joined them. "I need to talk to all of you."

Xander looked up as Felicity closed the last box of the game.

"I won! I finally beat you!" She jumped up and hopped around Xander, clapping and squealing in delight.

Getting to his feet, Xander gave Felicity's hair a good-natured ruffle. "Great job, kid." His gaze turned to Sabine. "What's up?"

"I'm going to the surface, back to RaShell, to be specific—"

"But you'll get in trouble for kidnapping us." Felicity settled immediately, crossing her arms and chewing her bottom lip.

Neriah flung herself at Sabine, wrapping her arms around her knees and hanging on tight. "You said we never had to go back!"

"Oh sweetie, you aren't going back. Just me." She

patted the top of Neriah's head. "I need to talk to Gavin."

"He won't like you returning without us," Aria said with a frown.

"I have some good news for him." Sabine opened her arms to the two older girls, who took the invitation and hugged her. "It'll be fine, you'll see. He's going to be happy when he finds out you all don't have to have babies now. And Xander will be here with you, keeping you all safe." She met his gaze, and though he frowned, he nodded. "Why don't you lot go get ready for bed while Xander and I talk for a minute?"

Aria stepped away and took Neriah by the hand. "C'mon, if we hurry there might be time for one more game of dots and boxes."

Sabine waited until the girls were out of sight, then motioned to the fire. "Come join me? We need to go over some things."

"You sure about this?" he asked without preamble. "I don't like the idea of you going alone."

"I don't like it either, but I can't leave the girls here by themselves and I can't take them with me." She held her palms toward the flames, enjoying the warmth. "That doesn't leave a lot of options."

"What if we took them to Marina? Maybe we could leave them with her and the other kids. That way I could go with you."

Sabine shook her head. "She's due soon, and

besides, not everyone down here likes the girls. I mean, there's no hiding they're albinos, and it's common knowledge they're from the surface, but only Dalton knows they're genetically engineered. It would only take one person to figure it out and spread the word. They need protection and looking after."

"You're right." Xander got up and grabbed the canteen. After taking a long drink, he passed it over. "How sure are you Gavin will listen?"

Accepting the offered water, she drank before answering. "He's invested a lot into the RaShell clones, and even more into genetically engineering all the girls to mature quickly and have babies. He really does want to save the planet. As awful as it is that R1 and her baby died, I hope that loss will open his mind to the possibility of healing the surface with the lake water." She screwed the lid back on the canteen and set it by her feet. "I have to try to make him see this is the way."

Xander nodded, though his frown was still in place. "When will you leave?"

"First thing in the morning."

Seven

Xander gave Sabine the mask and a few other essentials he'd brought with him on his trek to the cavern, while Aria hung three canteens of lake water from the traveling pack. Taking the data logbook from Felicity, he stuffed it into a zippered pouch in the pack, separate from the rest of her supplies.

Neriah tugged on his sleeve. "Now?"

Smiling, he nodded. "Now."

The littlest of the girls held up a small cloth bag. "Dried fish and carrots, in case you get hungry."

Sabine knelt in front of Neriah and drew her into a hug. "Thanks! You're so thoughtful. That'll help me a lot, kiddo."

Felicity and Aria joined in the hug, while Sabine looked up and gave him a slight nod.

"C'mon you three," he said, "time for her to get moving. And we're going to go see Dalton."

At the mention of the man's name, the girls twittered like a little flock of chicks, excited and happy.

Sabine got to her feet, and to his surprise, hugged him, too. "Keep them safe, no matter what."

"I will." Feeling a bit awkward, he patted her back. "I promise."

ﮂ ﮂ ﮂ

Sabine stood at the entrance to the cavern and adjusted her mask and goggles for the final time. She couldn't see the land beyond yet, as the cave was hidden by a scattering of boulders, but she knew what was out there.

Nothing.

Barren landscapes, dried up rivers, and polluted lakes. She glanced at the sky, a flat, dull gray, same as it'd been for years now. When she was a girl, one could gauge the time by looking at the sun in the sky. Though the sun was still there, hidden somewhere in the haze, those days were long gone.

Taking a deep breath, Sabine hitched her pack higher on her shoulders and left the cave.

A wave of heat blasted her face. With no healthy

trees or vegetation, the temperatures soared. By the time she came out from behind the final jagged boulder and into the desolation stretched before her, beads of sweat had already popped up on her forehead.

"Two days," she muttered. "Easy peasy."

Her feet stirred clouds of dust as she walked, and within minutes, her pant legs and boots were coated in a thick layer of grime. Thoughts of what the world could be like once restored to its former bounty occupied her mind as she trekked toward the first landmark.

Food would be plentiful, water would be clean and pure, and the world would be filled with the joyous sound of children laughing. The air would be safe to breathe, the animal mutations a relic of this soon-to-be-forgotten world.

She couldn't wait.

The Three Sisters came into view. The trio of towering hoodoos—tall, skinny spires of rock—stood majestic against their dull surroundings. Protruding from the ground in a cluster of three, their once deep, rust red color had faded to a pale rosy pink. They were the prettiest things left in this part of the natural world, and her gaze wandered to them often as she passed by.

Her thoughts turned to RaShell Bionics as she walked, to Gavin and his wife Liliam and the tragic loss of their only beloved child, an albino daughter named Rachelle, when she drank toxic water. In his grief, Gavin used her DNA to make his first-generation clones, the RaShell, or "R" models, and later, the second generation, like Aria, Felicity, and Neriah.

The idea of genetically engineered children who could reproduce had been brilliant thinking on his part, and she, along with a handful of other top geneticists, had helped design the children with cutting-edge bio-technology. They'd implanted fertilized but dormant embryos which would trigger and result in active pregnancies when the clones reached the maturity of a sixteen-year-old. With the double-time accelerated growth and maturation rates of the engineered children, the population problem was on target to be resolved within two generations.

Except…the R1 clone and her baby died.

Up ahead, Sabine saw the dead and decaying remains of the Joshua Tree Forest and stopped for a rest. Once she found a place to sit, she removed her pack and arranged a canteen, a piece of dried fish and half a carrot in her lap. She took off her jacket, zipped and snapped it up securely, then tugged the drawstring at the neck, closing the opening nice and snug. Finally, she pulled the jacket over her head and torso, tucked the bottom hem into her waistband, and took off her mask and goggles.

Just enough of the dull, natural light filtered in for her to see as she ate her snack. She finished with a hearty swig of the rejuvenating lake water in the canteen, which would restore any damage she'd endured while not wearing her mask.

A few moments later, protective gear back in place, and jacket removed, she glanced around at the dead landscape. She'd need to be careful not to lose her way through the Joshua trees. Everything looked the same, with one exception—the Great Divide on her left.

The Divide itself was a steep drop-off into Devil's Canyon, with razor sharp rocks, ravines, enormous boulders at the bottom, and endless trails of parched earth. The edge was almost impossible to see as it blended against the horizon with the land on the other side, creating an optical illusion of flat, unobstructed ground. If she looked carefully, though, every so often she'd see piles of rocks stacked about waist high, placed there by travelers to mark the dangerous boundary of the divide.

The other side of the Joshua Tree Forest was her halfway point, though with no way to know how much day was left, she didn't know if she'd make it before darkness fell. One thing was for certain, crossing in the dark was not an option.

Readjusting her goggles and mask, she double-checked to be sure the fit was tight, then settled her pack into place. She set out into the remnants of the Joshua trees, keeping a brisk pace and a careful eye out for the rock piles to her left.

The already dull light began to fade, and she looked for a good place to stop for the night. She made camp at the base of what'd been a tall Joshua tree but was now bent and half-rotted. Setting her pack down, she gathered small rocks for a firepit and some larger ones for a backrest against the dead tree. By the time it was dark, she had a cheerful blaze burning and was resting comfortably.

Logic told her it was silly to have a fire when she didn't need it to cook, but her soul needed the warmth and the inviting crackles of dead wood burning were a balm to her ears. She replicated her jacket-dome from earlier and ate the rest of the carrot and two pieces of dried fish, then polished off one of her three canteens. The lake water, along with a few samples stored in her pack, would serve to replicate her experiments for Gavin.

It was risky, she knew, since he was sure to have her arrested for kidnapping the instant she showed her face at the facility, but she also knew with the death of R1, he'd be growing desperate.

She prayed he'd listen to her long enough for her to show him how the water from Fertile Lake could save the world.

৩ ৩ ৩

Xander lay on the extra cot at Sabine's camp, staring up at the rock ceiling. The air was different—lighter, thinner, while the darkness was denser. He hadn't seen stars for years, but on the surface, the sky seemed far away rather than close, like the ceiling did here. It was a bit unsettling.

His gaze went to the firepit. The flames had long since died down and Aria had banked the fire for the night before going to bed, leaving nothing but a reddish glow to break the dark. After only a day, he was nowhere near accustomed to the rhythm of life underground. He felt out of whack, his inner clock totally off, and his sleep cycle disturbed.

He rolled over and, in the near pitch dark, could barely make out three heads of pure white hair. These girls were remarkable. At first glance, they seemed almost like ordinary kids, barring their striking appearance. After the day he'd spent with them, though, it was obvious they were special. Smart, clever, with problem-solving skills that belied their tender ages.

He recalled with vivid clarity seeing the R1 model back at RaShell Bionics, her eight-year-old body with a pregnancy bump showing. The sight shocked him. She'd wandered into the cafeteria one day while he was eating lunch. Silence descended over the crowded room as she made her way to the front of the line and asked for some ice cream. Only a moment later, Gavin and two doctors arrived to escort her back to wherever she'd come from with good-natured smiles, but no explanations.

There'd been rumors, of course, of Gavin breeding his clones, but no one really knew what that meant. When he'd next seen Sabine, he asked her about the girl and she told him of their accelerated maturity and how the eight-year-old was actually a sixteen-year-old girl and that, while still young, a prime age for childbearing. Geneticists had engineered the fetuses to develop smaller than average to accommodate the young bodies of their host. She'd gone on to give him a bare outline of Gavin's plan to address the declining population.

While he'd certainly been in awe of the ambitious plan, he'd also been skeptical and more than a little troubled. The biggest thing he couldn't wrap his mind around was children bearing children. The science behind it was solid. It was the sight of it that didn't, couldn't, reconcile in his brain.

His gaze landed once more on the trio of white-haired girls, and a slight shudder ran through him at the thought of Aria pregnant.

Sleep was a long time coming that night.

Eight

abine woke to the dull, dreary sky casting a grayish hue over the Joshua Tree Forest. Her fire had died off during the night, leaving her nothing to do except huddle under her jacket-dome for breakfast. She finalized preparations, then got up to relieve herself before setting out.

As she was squatting behind the remnants of the dead tree, gripping the trunk for balance, she felt a trio of sharp stings on the back of her hand.

With a yelp, she stared in disbelief. A large black scorpion sat on her hand, its three tails embedded in her flesh. She shook her hand violently and scrambled to her feet, nearly losing her balance as she struggled to yank her pants up.

"Shit!" Shaking, she inspected the wounds. The flesh was already going numb, which surprised her. She'd been stung once as a child, and it'd taken hours for the symptoms to settle in. But this scorpion was different. The three tails were a mutation that delivered triple the venom, if the rapid swelling in her hand was anything to go by.

She wanted to look for the little bugger, bag it as a sample and take it with her to study, but it'd already scurried away. Impatiently, she went to collect her backpack, reaching for a canteen of the lake water to heal herself. She unscrewed the cap, then paused.

What if she waited? What better way to show Gavin firsthand what the water from Fertile Lake could do? She'd be at RaShell by tonight. Surely, she could hold out that long. And if her symptoms got too bad and she couldn't wait, well, she'd have to treat herself along the way. There were the other samples to show him. Her original plan to prove her hypothesis was correct, was still valid.

Cradling her hand against her chest, she set out for RaShell.

ʒ ʒ ʒ

Xander woke the girls early—at least, he *thought* it was early—who could really tell with no clocks, and the only natural light filtering in from a fissure in the rock ceiling above the lake. The light glistened over the crystal-clear water of Fertile Lake, but it didn't do much to brighten Sabine's campsite.

He'd stoked the fire back up and, unsure what else to do about breakfast, got some hardtack soaking.

Aria was the first to join him by the fire. "What're you doing?" she asked, gesturing to his attempt at the morning meal.

He shrugged. "I didn't see anything to eat around here."

"We usually go to The Square to get our rations, or to Dalton's. Sometimes he has some fresh produce to share," she explained.

"Ah, well, we can't let this go to waste." He glanced at the bowl of unappetizing half-soaked biscuits, then back at Aria. "I can run to The Square though, get something to go with it."

"They probably won't have the ration booth open yet," she told him. "I'll go to Dalton's. If I hurry, I can be back before my sisters are asking for breakfast."

Anxious to explore more of the cavern, he stood. "How about we all go? You can show me around The Square on our way back."

"Okay!" Aria grinned and scampered off. "Felicity! Neriah! We're going to Dalton's!"

Sabine trudged along, her worry growing as her symptoms worsened. By the time she reached the other side of the Joshua Tree Forest, her hand was swollen twice its normal size, she was numb almost to her shoulder, and the entire arm twitched relentlessly. Her mask felt soggy from drooling and her clothes clung uncomfortably as the sweating increased.

"Gotta keep going," she muttered, the swelling in her throat and the thickness of her tongue distorting her words.

Thirsty…she was so thirsty. Tempted as she was to drink from her canteen, she also knew the worse her symptoms got, the more dramatic her healing would be, and she *needed* Gavin to believe her.

The desert stretched before her, harsh and unyielding. In the distance, shimmering like a mirage, were tall white buildings. But it was no mirage. It was RaShell Bionics. She recalled the walk from there to the Joshua trees taking half a day, though she suspected it might take longer in her current state. Still, she'd be there before dark.

Picking a landmark, a cluster of rocks surrounded by dead brush, she kept walking. She'd reevaluate her condition once she got there.

"Dalton!"

All three girls raced ahead when Dalton's shack came into view. The man himself stood at the door.

Xander waved and picked up the pace, joining them a minute later. It was a relief to see the man's wild gray hair and scruffy beard were as he remembered. Though it'd been only yesterday since he'd seen Dalton, his memory of the meeting was fuzzy. "Hey, man, how are you?"

Dalton stretched out a hand, and after a quick handshake, hugged the girls. "I'm good, just on my way to feed the animals." He grinned as he tousled Neriah's white hair. "What are you three up to this morning?"

"We're hungry!" Neriah exclaimed, her small face hopeful as she looked up at him. "Sabine had to leave, and Xander doesn't know how to make breakfast."

"Is that right?" Dalton chuckled and motioned to a basket on the ground. "Best get to work then. I'll milk Betty and you girls collect the eggs."

"What can I do?" Xander asked, taking off his jacket and rolling up his sleeves.

"Ever mucked a stall?" Dalton's eyes sparkled as he nodded to the small hut with a thatched roof across from his dwelling.

"No, but I'm a quick learner," Xander said, "and more than willing to earn our keep."

Dalton grabbed a pail from a stump by his front door. "I appreciate that, friend."

Following the older man, Xander was soon inside the makeshift barn, pitchfork in hand.

There were four small pens—a pair of goats was in the first one—and Dalton picked up a stool and sat on it, milking a goat while Xander moved on to the next stall. Inside that one was a pig, while the remaining two held a donkey and a sheep.

"Move that wheelbarrow over and clean everything out of each stall—hay, poop, and any spilled feed," Dalton instructed. "It all goes to the compost pile for the crops. Then lay down some fresh hay and that's it."

Starting at the far end, Xander entered the pen with the sheep first.

"You been at RaShell long?" Dalton asked, his voice slightly muffled.

"A couple of years." Xander scooped a forkful of manure into a waiting wheelbarrow, wrinkling his nose at the smell. Still, it smelled more natural than anything on the surface, so he could appreciate that.

"I worked there for a while, quite a few years back. Did Sabine tell you that?"

Xander's ears perked up. "She never said anything. What did you do there?"

"Same thing as Sabine, I was a geneticist."

"Why'd you leave?"

A soft *thud* sounded from Dalton's stall, followed by a string of curse words.

"You okay?"

"Damn goat kicked me. She's an ornery old thing."

Xander suppressed a chuckle as Dalton cussed again. A scraping sound came from the stall, then a few bleats from the goats before things settled.

"Now where were we?" Dalton asked, his voice more muffled than before.

"You were going to tell me why you left RaShell."

"Ah yes, well, I saw what Gavin had in mind after his daughter died. At first, I thought it was the answer. He's very convincing, you see. I did think it odd that he wanted all the clones to look like Rachelle, but grief does things to a person, and I'm not one to judge." More shuffling sounded, then Dalton continued, his voice clearer this time. "But then I heard the rumors."

"Rumors?" Xander, now finished with the sheep's stall, moved on to the donkey's enclosure. "Rumors of what?"

"An underground lake surrounded by a settlement. I had to come see for myself if the rumors were true. The thing about rumors, though, they're vague. This one, especially. Of course, now I know it was to protect the people here. It took me almost a year of searching to find this place."

"A year!" Xander scraped the soiled hay and droppings into a pile and scooped it into the wheelbarrow, thinking of his own journey here. Sabine had given him very specific directions with landmarks to follow.

"I was only the second outsider to find Fertile Lake and its inhabitants. The first man, when he finally made it back to RaShell, was delirious, spouting nonsense about the caves, tunnels, babies, and magic water. Everyone took him for confused, even brain-damaged, after his time outside unprotected. Not me, though. I heard a truth to his words, things that made sense from a scientific perspective."

"Like what?" Xander moved to the pig's stall, pulling his shirt over his nose at the stench.

"Like water from underground being pure, for one thing. It's always been a known fact that untainted sources produce untainted resources. All it takes is a few people to know that, to come someplace like this, and establish a settlement. I'd be willing to bet there are other places like this one in the world."

Xander finished up with the pig stall and laid some fresh hay down, then joined Dalton in the final enclosure.

"Wait 'til I'm done here," Dalton said, still milking the goat.

Nodding, Xander leaned against the gate. "Did you know Sabine before?"

"We worked in the same lab. She knew about the rumors too, and when I left and didn't come back, she eventually came looking. I was hoping she would. She's one of the brightest among the geneticists." Dalton sat up and moved the pail out of the way, then patted the goat on the rump. "Sabine is determined, if anyone can talk some sense into Gavin, show him there's another way now, it'll be her."

Just then, Felicity skipped into the barn. "Aria says I should come get you. We got all the eggs and the chickens are fed!"

Getting up from the stool, Dalton grabbed the pail and handed it to Felicity. "Take this inside and be careful not to spill."

The little girl took the pail by the handle and walked away, each step taken with exaggerated care.

Dalton shook his head as he reached for a rake. "Let's get this one cleaned so we can go eat."

ﭺ ﭺ ﭺ

Sabine collapsed, knees hitting the dirt as she braced herself against a rock. She'd made it to the landmark, barely. Her vision was so blurry, it seemed as if everything around her was an endless sea of indistinct gray and brown blobs.

She wasn't going to make it to RaShell in this condition. Not without some lake water. She struggled to remove her backpack, feeling tangled and clumsy as the straps refused to yield under her shaking hands.

Maybe if she just lay down and rested, caught her breath…

Falling over on her side, she tucked one arm under her head and cradled the injured one against her chest. She just needed to close her eyes for a minute, then she'd find the strength to retrieve the canteen. The ground was warm beneath her, the heat lulling her to sleep.

Somewhere in the distance, a horn sounded…a motor revved…voices shouted…

The hard ground disappeared, and she was floating.

A handful of words echoed in her mind.

"Get her to RaShell…"

Nine

"Nasty little buggers, those scorpions. Good thing my patrol found you."

Sabine opened her eyes to find Gavin standing at the foot of her bed, hands in the pockets of his suit pants, his expression unreadable. Her gaze darted around the room; white walls, white floor, no windows, and a single chair beside the hospital bed she was laying in.

She groaned as she tried to sit up, her muscles stiff and aching.

A nurse scurried in, raising the back of the bed for her.

Gavin gave the woman a terse nod, his gaze returning to Sabine. "Where are my girls?"

"Wher—" Her voice croaked, and her mouth felt like it was full of cotton. She cleared her throat. "Where's my pack?"

Gavin's eyes narrowed and a long pause stretched before he answered. "I had your pack searched. There was nothing of value in there."

"You're wrong," she said, her words raspy, but firm. "There's something more valuable than you can imagine."

Jaw clenched, he stepped to the end of the bed, leaned over, and gripped the rails. "Where. Are. My. Girls?"

She shook her head. "They're safe. I need to show you something, then we'll talk about them." Moving her legs, she tried to swing them over the edge of the bed, only to find she couldn't. She reached for the blanket and couldn't move her arm, either. "What—"

Gavin stepped forward and pulled the blanket down to reveal the cuffs around her wrists and ankles. "You didn't really think I'd trust you after what you did?"

Sabine glared at Gavin. "Please, just bring me my pack and let me show you what I came here to share with you, then I'll tell you everything."

He stared at her for a long moment, then without a word, went to the door and poked his head out. Her pack was handed to him, and the door clicked closed again.

Crossing the room, Gavin dropped the pack at the

foot of the bed and raised an eyebrow.

"The canteen," she said, nodding to the strap at the bottom where it was tied.

"Which one?"

"Doesn't matter."

Gavin's gaze darted back and forth between her and the canteen as he untied it. "You know you're under arrest, right?"

"I figured," she acknowledged. "But you might change your mind when you see what's in there."

Frowning, he removed the lid and sniffed, then peered inside. "Water? That's going to change my mind? Not likely."

"What did you give me for that scorpion sting?"

"Stuck you with an Epi, then some antihistamines and pain meds. Your hand is still swollen as fuck, though. That'll take some time to go down." He glanced at the canteen again. "What're you trying to pull here?"

Sabine grinned. "You're going to have to help me. I need to drink some of that water."

Gavin moved to her side and pressed the opening to her lips. "You understand I'm only indulging this nonsense because I want my girls back?" At her nod, he tipped the canteen, letting the water flow into her mouth.

After gulping several big swallows, she nodded.

He pulled the bottle away and replaced the lid. "So...now what? You're not thirsty anymore?" He leaned over the edge of the bed until he was almost nose to nose with her. "Talk."

Sabine closed her eyes, a smile tugging at the corners of her lips as she visualized the healing water flowing through her body and into her hand.

Shoving away from the bed, Gavin paced the room, the soles of his shoes tapping with each heavy step. "This is unacceptable! We had an understanding!"

Within moments, the pain was receding, the tightness of her flesh lessening. She felt her smile grow even as Gavin raged. Finally, she opened her eyes and looked at her hand. Her skin was significantly less mottled, and she could wiggle her fingers with ease. "Do you see this?"

"See what?" he shouted. Stomping to her bedside, he leaned over, his narrowed eyes glaring at her hand.

Sabine waited, filled with amusement and excitement as his expression changed. The scowl on his face relaxed, and his eyes widened. He reached his hand out and touched hers, stroking the flesh almost reverently.

"How?" His eyebrows furrowed. "What was in that water?"

"I don't know," she admitted. "I only know it heals people, plants, the soil, everything."

He snatched his hand away as his gaze shot to her. "And where did you get this 'healing water', or whatever you want to call it?"

She hesitated a moment. "I really can't say. Not yet anyway."

"And why not, pray tell?"

Well shit... He was back to being angry. "Because I can't. But I will, after we run some tests and find out more about it. I have an idea we may be able to use it though, to heal and replenish things, get back to normal. RaShell could do that instead of—"

"Instead of what? Repopulating the earth? Saving our species?" Gavin scoffed as he ran a hand through his hair. "I'm doing important work here, *groundbreaking* work. I'll not put that aside for some 'magic water'. RaShell is the *future*. I thought you understood that."

"It can still be the future, just in a different way than you envisioned. A better way." She watched as a whole spectrum of emotions crossed his face: disbelief, anger, grief, contempt, and smugness. She found she almost didn't want to say it, but it needed to be said. "The girls, and the rest of the clones, they don't have to have babies, Gavin. They don't."

He took a step back, his body rigid, his glare piercing. After a tense moment, he strode to the door and flung it open. "Lock her up," he said, as he stalked from the room.

Xander and the girls spent the whole morning at Dalton's, first eating a hearty breakfast of scrambled eggs, milk, and potatoes, then went to work in his vegetable garden.

"This all works because everyone contributes in one way or another," Dalton explained. "A large portion of my vegetables are donated and handed out every other day to all citizens who go to The Square for daily rations."

"What do they hand out the other days?" Xander asked, his curiosity about The Square growing.

"Bread, and once a week, meat, either rat or fish." Dalton passed out cotton-tipped swabs to Xander and the girls. "We're all going to be busy little bees today."

"Bees?" Aria questioned, accepting the swab with a frown. "This isn't a bee."

"It is today," Dalton said with a grin. "We've got to pollinate these plants, so more vegetables will grow."

Xander took Neriah's hand to stop her pulling the tip of her swab off. "Want to be my helper?"

"Yes!" she piped up. "But I don't know what we're doing."

Dalton laughed. "Hold your horses and I'll show you." He took his swab and swirled it around inside of a blossom on a nearby plant, then swabbed the blossom next to it, then the next. "These are a new crop of potatoes and since we don't get bees down here, we need to pollinate them ourselves so we have food to share."

Felicity scrunched her brows together as she watched Dalton. "How do you know if it works?"

"I know because I get potatoes. The ones we ate for breakfast came from my last crop." He moved to the next plant. "C'mon now, let's get busy. I still have to take vegetables to The Square today."

Xander kept hold of Neriah's hand and went to the row next to Dalton's. Following the other man's lead, he and his helper worked on their row while Felicity and Aria worked on the other side of Dalton.

Once they had the potatoes finished, they each got new swabs and moved on to the turnips. The morning sped by as they pollinated everything that had a blossom.

"Mind if we join you when you go to The Square?" Xander asked, as he helped Dalton load up vegetables in the wheelbarrow. "I haven't seen it yet."

"The more, the merrier," Dalton said, wiping a hand across his brow.

"I don't want to go." Neriah went to Aria and buried her face in her sister's side.

"Why not?" Xander lifted a brow at the older two girls, wondering what the problem was. Sabine had said they all liked going to The Square.

"It's because of Iver. He was mean to her yesterday," Aria explained.

"Mean? How?" Dalton looked back and forth between the girls. "Did something happen?"

Aria sighed, her reluctance obvious, but she finally told them what had happened with the ribbon. "Sabine said she was going to go back and make it right with him, but she never did."

"Ah…" Dalton relaxed, a half-smile lifting on one side of his mouth. "I'll take care of it."

"Thanks, man," Xander said, relieved at Dalton's offer of assistance. "I wouldn't know how to make amends with him. I've got to get my bearings down here so I can be of use."

"Nothing like a crash course to speed that along." Dalton chuckled, then motioned to the wheelbarrow. "Who wants to drive?"

Ten

This was a part of RaShell Sabine had never seen. She paced around and around in the tiny room, though 'room' was a vast overstatement. It was a cell. A ten-by-ten cell with a mattress on the floor, a toilet in the corner, and a jug of water by the solid steel door.

Gavin wouldn't keep her here long, though. He wanted to know where the girls were and, she hoped, he was curious about how the water in her canteen had healed her. No, he would just keep her here until he cooled off, then he'd be back.

The Square was everything Xander imagined and

more. The bustling center of the underground settlement boasted stalls lining the perimeter, with everything from clothing to earthenware dishes, woven baskets, and food for trade. There was even a booth offering hot beverages.

The man in question, Iver, was the proprietor of a stall full of ribbons, thread, and other sewing supplies. Xander and the girls hung back while Dalton spoke with the man.

"Should we go get rations?" Xander asked Aria.

"Let's wait for Dalton. He has to take his stuff since that's what he trades with," she replied.

"And what about us? What do we trade with?"

"We just tell them Sabine sent us," Felicity said.

"That's it? And they give you rations?" He frowned. Surely it wasn't that simple.

"Sabine made a deal with the community council," Dalton said, rejoining them. "She didn't tell you?"

"She said she takes care of any and all medical needs," Xander said. "Is there more than that? There is, isn't there? There has to be."

"There's more," Dalton agreed. He gripped the handles of his wheelbarrow and nodded across The Square. "Let's get this to the rations booth and I'll fill you in."

Xander walked with Dalton while the girls skipped ahead, laughing, and pointing at items of interest as they went. Keeping one eye on Neriah, Xander turned to Dalton. "So, what was the deal she made?"

"She's a geneticist, it's what she does, same as me. We're working on a project together to try to isolate the healing properties of the lake water. If we can, and if it can be replicated—"

"The world can be rebuilt—yeah, I know. There's nothing secret about that. She told me that's what she wanted to do. It's why she went to see Gavin after we tested the soil samples." Xander shook his head. "Unless...she didn't have proof until I got here, did she?"

"Nope." Dalton grinned as he tapped a finger on his temple. "Now you're thinking, putting it together. See, we couldn't get enough samples from anywhere but right outside the cave, not without exposing ourselves to the toxins. And while it's true we could drink the water to heal, we had to have samples from further away, and a wider variety. You did that for us."

"And the council? What's in it for them?"

"They own the lake." Dalton paused, an eyebrow raised as he cast a meaningful glance Xander's way.

"Money..." Xander sighed, his frustration rising. "It's about them getting the credit and the money. They're no different from Gavin—"

"Now, hold on a second there," Dalton said, stopping in the middle of the thoroughfare. "That's not true at all. They want to see the world healed as much as we do. You think we like living down here? You think this place is the future? The council wants say over when and how the lake is used, so it's not destroyed."

Realization dawned on Xander. "That's why you want to replicate the lake water, to preserve the source."

"Now you've got it." Dalton nodded and lifted his end of the wheelbarrow again, setting a brisker pace.

"Girls," Xander called, noticing they'd stopped at a booth up ahead.

"The ration booth," Dalton explained, steering toward it. "C'mon, let's see what we can trade for today."

ვ ვ ვ

Sabine didn't have to wait long. Though she had no way to tell the time, or even if it was day or night, she hadn't even been in here long enough to need to pee when Gavin came back.

A young orderly followed him in with two folding chairs, and after setting them up, left the room, locking the door behind him.

Gavin motioned for her to sit, then handed her a bottle of water and a sandwich wrapped in parchment paper.

Sabine accepted the items and sat, setting both on the floor next to her, and folding her hands in her lap.

From Gavin's slack expression and drooping shoulders, she knew something was wrong. "What is it?" she asked gently.

Silence stretched between them before he issued a heavy sigh. "R2 has given birth earlier than anticipated. Neither she nor the child survived."

"What happened?" she asked, reeling from the news.

He stared at her for a long moment. "When R2s programming terminated, it killed the child too. That's all you need to know."

"Oh no, I'm so sorry to—"

"Spare me your condolences," he snapped. "If you cared at all, you'd never have left, and you certainly wouldn't have stolen three of my girls."

Her heart ached for the loss of another clone and its baby. She had to make him see, make him understand. "I did care—do, I mean—I *do* care. That's why I came back, to show you—"

"Show me what? Magic water that can supposedly heal the world? What proof do you have? A soil sample, just one, and in an uncontrolled environment? That's not proof, Sabine. Surely you know that."

"Ah, you've been reading my notes," she said, pleased. "So, what about my scorpion sting? You saw that heal with your own eyes. How can you deny that evidence?"

"I didn't see you obtain that water, and I haven't seen the source. You could have put something in it, and how would I know?"

"Put something in it?" She frowned. "Like what?"

He waved a hand, dismissing the subject, then stood and raked his fingers through his hair. "Why did you need the girls, anyway? Why take them? What do they have to do with your soil samples?"

"I needed to test their blood, see what the water from the lake does when combined with their blood. See if it can heal them, too."

"Heal them from what, exactly? They're clones, they're perfect."

"Except their babies are dying," she said softly.

Gavin stormed across the tiny room, then came back to stand behind his chair with his arms draped over the back. Features tight, and jaw clenched, he said, "Only two now. Two babies have died."

"And how many unsuccessful pregnancies? Fertilized embryos that didn't implant? Miscarriages?"

"That's privileged information, and since you left, you're not privy to it anymore," he said, his voice tight. Stalking to the door, he banged on it, then turned to give her one last look. "You threw away your chance to be part of RaShell Bionics when you kidnapped my girls. We'll have no further discussion until I get them back."

The door opened, and he was halfway through

when she spoke.

"I can't give them back if I'm stuck in here."

Xander and the girls spent the remainder of the day with Dalton, not returning to Sabine's campsite until it was time to cook the evening meal. Loaded with fresh vegetables from Dalton and a thick, crusty loaf of bread from the ration booth, he and Aria set about making stew while Felicity and Neriah played nearby.

"It's good they can be kids," Aria remarked as she worked on chopping carrots.

Xander looked up from where he was coaxing the embers into flames. "What about you? Aren't you still a kid, too?"

"Nah, not really. I've always helped look after the younger ones, well, for as long as I can remember, anyway." She brushed a strand of white hair out of her eyes and smiled at him. "There were a lot of us at RaShell, and the older ones would help take care of the younger ones. Training, they called it, for when we have our own babies."

Choosing to ignore the question of how she felt about her upcoming forced motherhood, he changed gears. "Is that how you got so close to Neriah and Felicity? From taking care of them?"

"Yes, see, they would assign us two to three

children of different ages, and we'd be responsible for them for half of each day and night. Felicity was assigned to me when she was two, after her other surrogate sister lost her eyesight—from a rare condition that affects those with albinism—and could no longer care for her." Aria cast a fond glance at the two girls playing tic-tac-toe in the dirt. "Neriah I've had since her creation."

"Creation…" Xander knew they were products of the geneticists in the labs at RaShell, but he'd given little thought to what that actually meant. His job had been to keep the place secure, and that was his area of expertise.

Aria shrugged and tossed the carrots into the pot. "The babies we'll have will be the first generation of their kind. Part clone and part organic, like me, but born, instead of created."

"That's pretty cool, I guess," he said, unsure what else he *could* say to her.

She grinned as she picked up an onion. "It's very cool."

Now the fire was roaring, he sat next to her and reached for a potato. "And who taught you to cook?"

"Sabine…"

Eleven

Sabine had no idea how much time had passed. Days, surely, maybe more. She slept, she ate a single sandwich and drank a glass of water when she woke and found them by her mattress on the floor, and she paced endlessly around her tiny cell.

No one spoke to her. Worst of all, Gavin hadn't been back. She was certain he'd want to know more about the water. It broke her heart to know she held the key to rebuilding the world, and he wasn't even interested.

After an indefinite loop of sleeping, eating, and pacing, the door opened, and Gavin strode in. As before, an orderly followed him in with two chairs, then disappeared.

Gavin motioned to a chair.

Taking a seat, she sat in silence, waiting to see what he wanted from her.

Several long moments stretched before he spoke. "I've been looking at the water you brought."

A thrill shot through her, and she raised an eyebrow.

"Despite not being able to confirm the source or purity, I ran a few tests myself, and you were right. There appear to be healing properties," he continued. "I keep asking myself, though, why did you need the girls? They don't need to be healed, they're perfect. So, what do you really want with them?"

Sabine sat up straight and met his gaze. "If they were perfect, they wouldn't be losing their babies. I may not know exactly *how* the water works, yet, but I do know it works. My goal was to expose them to the water, have them drink it regularly, which I've done. I've tested their blood, looking for any changes—"

"And what did you find?"

Being careful not to divulge too much about the settlement, she replied, "I only had access to a microscope, nothing else. But I can tell you, the cells I studied looked different, kind of like the soil samples I saw—healthier, fuller, more natural and organic."

"So, you need more equipment and a lab. Nothing

can be decided one way or another until we follow protocol." His lips drew into a thin line and wrinkles creased his forehead. "I know you're not going to take me to this lake, but what if I let you go? Do I have your word you'll bring the girls back here, along with a quantity of water samples, so we can do a proper analysis?"

"You would just let me go?" Sabine shook her head. "Seems unlikely you'd trust me enough to keep my end of the bargain."

"Why wouldn't I?" He crossed his legs and folded his hands atop his knee. "You risked your life to come here with the water and the data. You trusted me to believe you. And you say you want to help. I think you do."

She narrowed her eyes as she considered him. "You're saying you believe me?"

"Not only do I believe you, I want to help you."

"And all I have to do is bring the girls back, along with some water?"

"Yes," he stated.

She stifled a laugh at the absurdity of his approach. He must think her stupid. "Now, why on earth should I trust you after you locked me in here?"

Gavin sat back, looking pleased with himself. "Because that's the only way you're getting out of here. So, do we have a deal?"

By the next day, Sabine was packed and ready to leave. Gavin supplied her with food, water, and a new airtight mask, all of which she thoroughly checked for tracking devices and had come up clean.

He refused to let her see any of the other clones, citing 'security concerns', which she expected, but still, she had to ask. She'd been hoping to at least catch a glimpse of them, see them playing, assure herself of their well-being.

Gavin himself walked her to the front gate. "Safe travels, Sabine, we'll expect to see you in," his gaze searched her face, "a week or so?"

She gave him a rueful smile. "You know I can't say, so, let's just go with you'll see me soon."

Though disappointment flashed in his eyes, he nodded. "We'll see you soon."

Adjusting her mask one final time, she hitched her pack over her shoulders and set out on foot in the opposite direction of Fertile Lake.

"Someone's coming!"

Xander looked up from where he was carving utensils out of scraps of wood, relief and excitement flooding over him. Sabine. It had to be. She'd been gone nearly two weeks.

96

Aria, who'd been at Dalton's helping with the potato harvest this morning, ran into their campsite, breathless. "Dalton said…you need to…come now," she said, panting.

Having already set aside his carvings, Xander stood and sheathed his knife. "Is it Sabine? Is she okay?"

"I don't know. The person's head and face were covered." Aria eyed her sisters. "I'm to stay here…look after them until you or Dalton comes to get us."

Xander nodded and, after giving Aria a quick squeeze on the shoulder, set out to Dalton's, glad for his newly acquired knife, as it was his only weapon. The second he was out of sight from the girls, he broke into a run.

The scene at Dalton's was chaos. Word spread fast of the visitor, and Xander had to push his way through a crowd to see what was what.

Dalton knelt in the dirt, an unconscious man laid out before him.

Xander dropped to his knees beside Dalton. "Who is he? Do you know?"

"He didn't say before he passed out." Dalton motioned to the RaShell Bionics patch on the arm of the man's jacket. "I was hoping you'd recognize him."

Peering closer, Xander studied the man's features, then shook his head. "I have no idea, but RaShell is a huge place. I can tell you he wasn't security."

"How do you know?"

Xander glanced around, taking in the crowd, most of whom seemed to be listening intently. His gaze returned to Dalton. "Let's get him inside."

Moving to the man's head, Xander lifted him under the arms, while Dalton took his feet, and together they hauled him into the hut and laid him on the cot. The man didn't even stir.

"You were like this when you got here," Dalton remarked, nudging Xander's shoulder with his own, then nodding toward the small table across the room. "Come sit down and tell me what you know."

Sabine walked until RaShell Bionics was out of sight, then just in case anyone followed, she kept walking. Ahead was Devil's Canyon, and while it would add an entire day to her travels, she knew she could cut through, walk along the dried-up riverbed, and come out next to the Joshua Tree Forest.

She didn't believe Gavin wanted to help her. He wanted the girls back. Still, she had an opportunity to bring some water to a proper lab, run some tests, and maybe do something to make a better future. And if she was lucky, Gavin would see the light and help her in the end.

The further away from RaShell she got, the more

the terrain changed. Flat, dusty ground turned rocky, with cracks running along the parched surface. The dirt was so dry, her feet sunk between steps, leaving a clear trail in her wake.

Hopefully, the ground in the canyon would hide her tracks. And hopefully, no one was following her.

ک ک ک

"Every employee of RaShell has those patches on their uniforms," Xander said, sipping water as he spoke. "But different colored patches mean different things. Security has red patches. Green, like his, are for the greenhouse workers, yellow for the lab technicians, and blue for the geneticists, like Sabine."

Dalton nodded thoughtfully. "That's changed since I was there. They used to state the department on your ID badge, which you'd scan to enter your work area, along with a finger on a pad to verify identity."

"They did away with that system not long after you would've left. Now they use facial recognition and iris scans. The patches are just for show. Of course, there are overriding master keys, but…" Xander glanced over his shoulder at the still unconscious man. "I think Gavin's wife likes knowing who belongs where."

"Liliam never strayed far from the nursery," Dalton remarked, running his finger around the rim of his cup.

"She still doesn't. That's why the patches are

helpful." Xander eyed Dalton. "I hope Sabine's okay. I didn't expect her to be gone this long. When Aria said there was a visitor, I thought it was her."

Behind them, the man stirred. Both Xander and Dalton rushed to his side as the man was overcome with a coughing fit.

"Hey, take it easy now," Dalton said, helping the man sit up. "Xander, water please."

Hurrying to the bucket by the table, Xander dipped the ladle and filled a cup. "Here you go."

Dalton held the cup to the man's lips. "Drink up, it'll help."

The man alternated between coughing and sipping water, until a few minutes later, he finally settled. He looked around the tiny hut. "Where am I? Did I make it?" He looked at Xander square in the eye. "Am I at the lake?"

Flashing a quick look to Dalton, who nodded, Xander turned back to the man. "You are, you made it. Can you tell us who you are? Did Sabine send you?"

"Sabine? I don't know any Sabine. Trevor told me to come find Dalton." The man looked at Dalton. "Do you know where I can find him?"

"You're looking at him. What did Trevor say?"

The man fell silent and scratched his chin, presumably lost in thought. After a moment, he perked up. "He said to tell Dalton 'The chair is against the wall'.

Did I get that right?" His anxious gaze darted between the two men.

Dalton glanced at Xander. "That means there's trouble with Gavin." His gaze returned to the man. "What's your name?"

"Ruston. Did you just say Gavin is in trouble?"

"No, I said there's trouble *with* Gavin, there's a difference. Anything else?"

"I'm to tell you R2 and her baby have died. R3 is due any time now, but she's not doing well." Ruston coughed again, then drained his cup.

Xander reeled. *R2 died? How? When?* He got up and paced the room, his gaze darting to Dalton. "Do you think that's why Sabine isn't back yet?"

"Could be." Dalton frowned.

Xander was about to ask another question when Aria stuck her head into the hut. "The council is here."

Twelve

Sabine picked her way down the steep hillside leading into Devil's Canyon. Loose rocks and shale dislodged with each step, creating a slippery slide of pebbles, dirt, and debris beneath her feet. Using dead foliage and small boulders to hang onto, she managed not to lose her balance, but the going was painstakingly slow.

Keeping an eye out for snakes and scorpions, she finally reached the bottom. From here, all she had to do was follow the dry riverbed for about a day, assuming she kept a good pace, then hike her way back out.

She took out her canteen and had a quick drink, then adjusted her mask, which was already covered in a dusty film. Everything was parched, and she was soaked in sweat. It was going to be a very long day.

Xander went outside to find two men and a woman standing in a semicircle, waiting. All three had gray hair and wore long robes over their clothing. The crowd from earlier had grown, making the patch of ground around Dalton's nearly as bustling as The Square.

Dalton stepped forward, holding out a hand to the taller man. "Matthew." After a brief handshake, he moved on. "Ellen, Warren. This is Xander, and Ruston." He gestured to each of them in turn.

Matthew nodded politely, then clasped his hands in front of him. "We're here on official business, gentlemen."

"I see that," Dalton replied. "What can we do for you?"

"We were informed we have another visitor from RaShell," Warren said, looking directly at Dalton. "It's concerning how this is becoming a regular occurrence."

"You know the importance of keeping our location a secret," Ellen scolded. "The last thing we need is to be overrun with Gavin's cronies."

Xander was about to protest when he realized his former position in security would mean he'd likely be thought of as one of the 'cronies', so he kept his mouth shut.

"How are these people finding their way here?" Matthew asked, looking at Ruston and Xander.

Ruston stepped forward, but Dalton put his arm across the man's chest, stopping him. "I'll handle this," he muttered. Clearing his throat, he motioned to his hut. "Would you three like to come inside and we'll discuss in private?"

Warren, Ellen, and Matthew huddled a moment, whispering amongst themselves, then faced Dalton.

"Thank you," Warren said, "but no. This affects the safety of the residents, therefore, will be discussed publicly."

"As you wish," Dalton conceded. "In answer to your question, I'm responsible."

A murmur swept over the gathered crowd, and Matthew raised a hand, quieting them. "Continue, please."

"Before I left RaShell, I made a deal with one of the techs there. He'd keep an eye on things that might be of interest to me, and I gave him discreet directions on how to get here. We agreed upon a series of coded messages, so I'd know any visitors had been sent by him—"

"What things of interest?" Ellen said with a frown.

"Anything that might have a significant impact our lives down here, or theirs up there," Dalton said simply.

"Like what, specifically?" Warren asked.

Dalton filled them in on the dying pregnant clones

and the potential trouble with Gavin, and again, murmurs rose from the crowd.

The three council members formed a small huddle once more. Matthew addressed them, "What do you propose to do about the situation?"

ॐ ॐ ॐ

"You can't leave. Who's going to take care of us?"

Xander gathered Neriah into his arms for a big hug. "You and your sisters are going to stay with Dalton until I get back."

"What about Sabine? You're going to look for her, too, right?" Felicity stood holding Aria's hand, her small forehead creased with worry.

"I will look for her," he agreed.

"Why do you have to go?" Neriah said, her words muffled as she nuzzled his shoulder.

"The last of the original clones is about to have her baby, and she's sick. We don't know how much lake water it will take to make her better, so I'm going to bring her here so we can help her," he explained. Setting Neriah back on her feet, he drew Aria and Felicity into a two-armed hug. "Look after her and stay out of trouble."

"We will," Aria said.

"I packed some things for you," Dalton said, joining them. He handed a large backpack to Xander, followed by a gas mask. "I know you gave your equipment to Sabine, but you need to wear something out there. I reckon this will work."

"Thanks, man." Xander accepted the pack and inspected the contents. Four full canteens, a parcel of food, a first-aid kit, a flashlight, a change of clothes, and two lightweight blankets.

"In that zippered pocket you'll find matches, a small bundle of tinder, and an extra ration of hardtack. You remember the way? You were a bit of a mess when you got here."

"Yeah, I was, but my memory cleared as soon as the lake water healed me. I remember how to get there." Xander held out a hand to Dalton, and they shook firmly. "Thank you for taking care of the girls."

"No problem." Dalton grinned at the trio. "C'mon, you lot, we've got chores to do and Xander needs to get on his way."

Putting on the backpack, Xander gripped the gas mask in one hand and waved with the other. "I'll be back soon." With that, he turned and headed for the tunnel leading to the cave's entrance.

By nightfall, Sabine had reached the narrow end of Devil's Canyon and picked a spot to camp for the night. She made a small fire, then, using the same trick as before, domed her jacket around herself and ate the last sandwich Gavin had put in her pack. After tonight, it was dried food or ration bars for the rest of the trip. She ought to be sick of the sandwiches. She'd eaten the same thing since arriving at RaShell, but instead, she savored the chewy, crusty bread, the tangy sauce spread on both sides, the crisp bite of pickles, and the thick slices of salty cheese.

When she finished, she drank from her canteen, then secured her mask back in place and sat staring at the fire until her eyes were heavy.

Xander had left much later in the day than he'd have liked and only made it to the edge of the Joshua Tree Forest before the darkness forced him to stop for the night. He picked a spot amongst the dried-up corpses of the Joshua trees and got a fire going, then removed the parcel of food from his backpack. As he sat staring into the flames, he broke off bite-sized pieces of salted fish and slipped them under his gas mask, chewing slowly.

He still needed to figure a way into RaShell once he got there. It wasn't like he could just walk up to the front gate and knock. He'd deserted, after all, and was likely to be arrested if he was caught. The greenhouses, though, could be his way in. While the domed structures had security, there were also more access points, and he was confident he could sneak in. Once there, he'd simply watch and wait, see who might look friendly or see who was careless enough to leave an opening for him. It wasn't a great plan, but it was a place to start.

He put the rest of his food back into the pack, then using it as a headrest, stretched out on the hard ground and tucked in for the night.

The next morning, Sabine stood at the base of a steep cliffside, searching for the best way up. There was the faint outline of a trail, a remnant of days gone by, zig-zagging across the face, but the ground was littered with rocks and loose shale. She'd have to watch every step.

The going was easy enough at first, but before long, she was looking for handholds, and digging her feet in with every step as dirt and pebbles showered down the hillside in her wake. About halfway up, a large boulder jutted out, if she could just make it there…

Keeping her eyes trained on the boulder, she took another step and the ground beneath her feet fell away. She slid down on her stomach in a blur with debris tumbling around her. Scrambling for something to grab onto, she found purchase on a jagged stone embedded in the ground. Pain sliced across her palm, but she held tight as her heart pounded.

"Too fucking close," she muttered, dragging a ragged breath. She rested her head on her forearm for a moment. *Now what?*

Several moments passed before she looked up. She still had quite a way to go, and unless she wanted to be here during the hottest part of the day, she'd better get moving.

Tightening her grip on the stone, she ignored the searing pain and kicked her toes against the ground, digging in until she had footholds. She let go of the rock and surveyed the damage to her palm. A deep cut ran from one side to the other and dark crimson blood ran down her arm, drops plopping into the dirt. She gritted her teeth and kept going.

Inch by inch, one foothold after another, she crawled her way up. Only now, she took her time, digging in with every step. Her hand left a bloody trail, marking handholds she'd used with a big red blotch. With no one around to hear her, she cussed, screamed, and hollered her pain with each new grab.

By the time she reached her intended resting spot, her face was covered in sweat, snot, and tears, all clouding her vision inside her protective mask. She climbed to the top of the boulder and collapsed, trembling with a combination of adrenaline and exhaustion.

She closed her eyes as dry sobs of relief racked her

body. After a moment, she collected herself enough to sit up. She couldn't see a damn thing through her filthy mask, so she removed it. Setting it on the ground beside her, she slipped off her backpack, rummaging through the contents until she found her spare t-shirt. She ripped a length off the bottom and unhooked a canteen from her pack.

She had to work fast—each breath of toxic air was causing damage to her airways and lungs.

Pouring the only water she had over her cut, she used the remainder of the t-shirt to scrub the debris from the injured flesh. Once it looked clean, she splashed a bit more water over her hand and wrapped it with the strip of cloth.

She wiped the visor, then quickly mopped her face and replaced her mask. *I'd kill for some lake water right now.*

Scooting, she sat with her back against the hillside and shut her eyes. She needed to rest a few more minutes before making the last part of her climb.

Thirteen

Xander trudged through the Joshua Tree Forest for most of the day. By the time he reached the edge and could see the RaShell buildings in the distance, it was dark. After only a moment's hesitation, he decided to keep going. His goal was to sneak in through the greenhouses, and the cover of night would help.

He picked up the pace, jogging until he couldn't see to avoid any potential dangers, then he continued on at a brisk walk. Ahead and to the left, he saw the dim glow of the greenhouses, though it was hard to gauge the distance in the dark. He'd visited them once before, long enough to grab a soil sample, but hadn't had the time to explore.

Each glass building was roughly the length of a football field—something he remembered from his youth—and sat in five neat rows of ten. He slipped through a maintenance gate that'd been left ajar in the fence and as he approached the first row, he saw a few guards posted.

With nowhere to hide, he dropped to the ground and waited. He was close enough to hear they were talking, but only the occasional word drifted his way. Most of their conversation was muffled.

Soldier-crawling, he inched closer until the words were clearer.

"…why'd they send her out there? She's a new recruit. She ain't gonna know what to do—"

"That's why, dummy, because she's new. She won't be missed if she doesn't come back."

"That's a shit thing to do to her. She's young, inexperienced."

"Why do you care, anyway? You like her or something?"

"Nah, but I got a heart, man. She don't deserve to be served up like a lamb to the slaughter."

"You really think those people are dangerous?"

"Gavin said—"

"Yeah, yeah, Gavin said," the guard mocked. "He didn't even let Reed take a weapon when he sent her back."

Reed? Is that Sabine they're talking about? Xander moved closer, straining to get a better look at the two in the darkness.

"No weapon? Not even a knife? There's shit out there that'll kill her. You heard about that scorpion sting she had when she got here, right?"

"I saw it myself, was me and Blackburn who picked her up out there. Look, she'll be fine, and if she isn't, well, that newbie is following her, so I'm sure she'd help her out in a jam."

Shit...shit, shit, shit... Xander pressed his masked forehead to the ground in frustration. Sabine had already left and was being followed. His instincts screamed at him to go help her, keep her from inadvertently giving away the location of the caves, but then one of the men spoke again.

"You know R3 is gone now, right? You think Reed smuggled her out?"

"No fucking way. Reed was walked to the front gate by Gavin himself. Wherever R3 went, she did it on her own. Hell, she probably went out for a walk and got herself lost."

A disbelieving snort and then, "Poor thing wasn't looking too good after hearing the other two had died."

"They're just clones. Why do you even care, man?

"They're our future—"

"Well fuck, you really bought into all that shit, huh?

Gavin's got you believing no one but his clones can have babies—that our population is doomed? That dumbshit isn't looking in the right place is all."

Xander scooted closer, finally getting enough of a look to know the man who'd just spoken was short, a good foot shorter than the other guy.

"And where should he be looking?" the taller man asked.

The short guy shrugged. "Not for me to say."

The taller one turned away, and the conversation ceased.

ʒ ʒ ʒ

Sabine woke with a start. She had no way to tell time, but it felt late, much later than she would've liked. A memory flashed through her mind: her first job, her first sick day. Going home early, she'd meant to only nap for an hour, then get ready for a date with one of her co-workers (what was his name, anyway?) but she'd overslept, for hours. She'd woken with that groggy sense of having slept both too much and not enough and missed her date altogether. She had no memory of what ever happened to that guy, but waking like this now felt exactly like it had then.

Blinking, she looked around. Oh…right, she was halfway up the cliff face, resting on a boulder. She moved to get up, then winced as a spear of pain sliced through her hand. Glancing down, she saw the makeshift bandage was steeped in blood, dried and caked at the edges, and soggy in the middle.

"Fabulous," she muttered, reaching for her pack.

She didn't have time for much, but with her energy sapped, she ate a ration bar, then washed it down with the now warm canteen water. There were no clean bandages, or even anything she could use as a makeshift one, so she zipped her pack, then got to her feet.

"Don't look down, don't look down," she whispered as she looked down the mountainside. Her stomach lurched, and she swallowed hard against the rising bile. "Oh God…"

The only good news was, she'd made it more than halfway. But there wasn't much time before dark, and no room for error.

Stay the night here or climb?

She examined her hand again, wiggled her fingers, then shuddered at the resulting pain. It was probably the start of an infection. She couldn't stay.

Glancing up, her gaze followed the faint outline of the trail she'd been following, and she sighed. Time to go.

Using the same process as before, only this time, triple checking her hand and footholds, she slowly made her way up the side of the mountain. The top edge was within reach when the last of the light faded, leaving her in total darkness.

Heart pounding, she closed her eyes, visualizing the remaining distance. Carefully, and with abject terror, she reached for the ledge above her. She dug her fingers in, ignoring the now searing fire in her injured palm, then kicked her toes into the dirt one last time. Once her foot was secure, she pulled herself up, lifting her other leg over the edge. With the ground firmly under her, she rolled away from the cliff.

Laying on her side, she tucked her arm under her head and crashed.

Xander waited until the shift change, then made his move. With four guards convened around the back end of a truck, he slipped between the first two greenhouses. He didn't dare go into any in the first row, though, so sticking to the shadows, he crept to the third row. Knowing there were people employed around the clock, he huddled in the dark, waiting for his chance.

He got it when a door opened and someone in a pair of disposable, protective coveralls with a face mask stepped outside. The hydraulic door closed slowly enough, Xander slipped through unnoticed.

Once inside, he ducked behind a row of thriving greenery and peered out from between the leafy plants.

A few workers moved around, one sticking a finger

into various plant beds, then writing on a clipboard, while another was occupied with a section of pipe hanging from the ceiling. Two more were at a table near the back, planting seeds into tiny containers.

On the far side of the greenhouse was a long counter littered with coffee cups, papers, and a few scattered dishes. A corkboard hung on the wall with several sets of keys dangling from hooks along the top.

The keys were exactly what he needed. Though he didn't have his ID badge, his uniform or patch, and scanning his iris would be a suicidal move, a set of master keys would override the need for any of those things.

He duck-walked his way down the aisle, then stopped to be sure no one was looking before scurrying across to the row next to the counter. From here, he couldn't go any further until the worker checking the plants moved on.

Keeping a close eye on the person's boots, he slipped under the table and prepared to wait for as long as it took when an alarm rang out.

The worker dropped the clipboard and took off.

Peeking out from under the table, he watched as the remaining workers vacated the greenhouse.

What the hell?

With a sharp glance around, he rolled out from his hiding spot, then hurried to the counter, scanning the key rings until he found the one labeled 'master'. He grabbed the keys and stuffed them in his pocket. When he turned to go, a figure in the doorway stopped him cold.

"What do you think you're doing?"

Fourteen

Sabine woke to her hand throbbing in sync with her heart. The heavy beat thrummed a fiery heat in her palm, traveling up her arm, and radiating pain throughout her body. Groaning, she sat up and cradled her hand in her lap. She thought about unwrapping the makeshift bandage to check the cut, but with no clean wrappings and no way to treat the injury, she decided against it. Best thing she could do was get back to the lake.

Her body stiff and sore, she was slow getting to her feet, but managed. Looking around, she was relieved to see she'd been right about the detour leading to the Joshua Tree Forest. Behind her was the unyielding desert, and ahead, the forest of dead trees.

After nothing more than a few sips of water, she adjusted her pack and set out.

ع ع ع

Xander stared at the man blocking his exit. Tall, no weapon, head cocked to the side as if more curious than anything. He didn't seem like a threat. Xander took a few steps.

The man reached behind his back and pulled a gun. "I asked you a question."

Xander froze, lifting his hands part way up. His mind raced, trying to think of a good enough reason for him to have taken the keys. No one who was supposed to be here would need them to move freely through the complex, as the iris scanners would grant them access to the entrances. He issued a heavy sigh. "Look, I need to get inside."

The man lifted his gun higher, aiming at Xander. "Why?"

"I got news of R2's death. I have information that could help R3," he answered truthfully.

"Who the hell are you? And what information?"

"Xander Mitchell, I used to work—"

"About fucking time you got here." The man's expression relaxed, and he lowered the gun. "And you can thank your lucky stars it was me who found you, otherwise, you'd be dead."

Xander put his hands down, though he didn't move. His heart pounded as he tried to process what the man had said. "What do you mean, it's about time I got here? Who *are* you? How'd you know I was coming?"

"No time for questions right now. The cameras are only down for ten minutes. Come with me." The man turned and left.

With no other choice, Xander followed.

Sabine trudged through the remains of dead Joshua trees at a sluggish pace. She couldn't be sure without looking, but she suspected the infection was getting nasty. Her body was soaked in sweat, but she had the shivers, and the pain in her hand was now a white-hot streak of agony up to her elbow.

As much as she wanted to stop and rest, she had to keep going. The lake was her only chance at healing, not to mention she needed to get news of R2's death to Xander and Dalton.

Ahead, she spotted the remnants of a campfire, and her heart skipped a beat. This wasn't hers from her trip to RaShell. She knew because it was out in the open, with no large, dead tree to shelter against.

Getting closer, the scent of burnt wood invaded her nostrils, even through her mask. These remains were fresh. She glanced around but didn't see anyone or anything out of place. Whoever it was, was long gone…or hiding. The thought occurred she might have someone following her after all. Her fevered mind conjured images of a faceless person watching her from the edge of the cliff as she'd struggled through Devil's Canyon.

Her stomach churned as unease washed over her. With the condition she was in, she wouldn't be able to fight, or even run, if someone *was* following her.

She looked around once more, this time scrutinizing each dead tree, searching for signs of someone hiding, but again, found nothing. On the verge of panic now, she kicked dirt over the charred remains of the fire, then stopped to pick up a fist-sized rock. The bastard Gavin had sent her out here with no weapon.

Keeping a tight grip on the rock, she left. It was better than nothing.

ろ ろ ろ

Xander followed his guide out of the greenhouse and through a maintenance door on the side of the main building. Once inside, they kept a brisk pace as they moved silently through the halls to a door labeled 'supply closet'. When the door opened, though, there was an open hatch on the floor, and the man climbed down without delay.

Xander went after him, dropping into a large room.

A bank of computers sat along the far wall, while shelves of equipment lined another. There was a long, white table cluttered with papers, books, and electronics off to the side. Two women and a man were hunched over the table studying a map, while two more people sat watching computer monitors. No one looked up when they entered.

The man turned to Xander. "I'm Trevor, welcome to The Opposition."

"Trevor?" Xander gawked at him. "Dalton's Trevor?"

Trevor chuckled. "I mean, Dalton works for us, but yeah. That's how we knew you were coming. We've been monitoring the complex, waiting for you."

Xander shook his head. "How'd you know where I'd be?"

"We didn't. That's why I left several maintenance gates ajar around the complex. We've just been watching, and when I saw you, we immediately looped the footage for the previous sixty seconds, then erased you from the surveillance video. We had to turn the cameras off long enough for me to get to you and bring you here." Trevor gave him a considering look. "Let me guess…you're wondering how I knew you were coming at all, right?"

Nodding, Xander cracked a half-smile and shrugged. "As a matter of fact, I was."

"C'mere, you're going to love this." Trevor motioned to the table, where the three people there were now watching them. "Make sure you get someone to close those gates," he said to them. His gaze went to Xander, then he pointed to a small circuit board with a black rectangular box and a round button. "Check it out."

Xander frowned at the object. He'd never seen anything like it and had no idea what it could be. "What is it?"

"A Morse code generator."

Xander's gaze flicked to a grinning Trevor, then back to the object in question. "You've got to be shitting me."

This time, Trevor gave a deep and hearty laugh. "Dalton's idea, actually. He set it all up before he left."

"Crafty old man. He never said a word about it," Xander said, studying the device closely. He only had a vague idea of what Morse code even was.

"Well, he wouldn't," Trevor said. "In fact, I'm surprised he even mentioned me at all."

"He had to. The Council insisted."

"The Council?" Trevor sounded surprised. "Why would he tell them?"

Xander filled him in on what had happened when Ruston arrived with his news of R2. "That's why I came here, to get R3 out of here and see if the lake water can

126

save her and the baby. But I heard some guards talking about R3 being gone. Is it true?"

"Oh…well, fuck." Trevor pulled out a chair and motioned for him to sit. "About that…"

ڴ ڴ ڴ

By the time the dull light had faded, Sabine had reached the edge of the Joshua Tree Forest. In the distance on her left, The Three Sisters stood majestic against the near dark sky.

The pain from her hand radiated to her shoulder now, and she hoped she had one more day in her to make it to the lake and its healing waters. If she had blood poisoning, which she suspected she did, she might not have that long.

The ground ahead was flat and dry, and with her slowed pace, she was sure it'd be daybreak before she was anywhere near the cave. She wasn't worried about missing the entrance in the dark.

Removing her pack, she one-handedly dug out a ration bar and her canteen. She didn't even dare sit to rest, afraid she wouldn't be able to muster the strength to get up and going again. After finishing her meager meal, she wrestled the pack over her shoulders, agonizing streaks of fire jolting through her at the movements.

Lightheaded and swaying with fatigue, she set out

into the desert with only a rock as a weapon and the vague outlines of the towering hoodoos as her guide.

Xander rubbed a hand across his face, trying to absorb the news. R3 wasn't just randomly lost as suggested by the guards he'd overheard earlier—she was missing, gone over a day now. "Don't they have some way to track her? She's a clone, after all."

Trevor nodded. "She is, and she does have an implanted tracking device. But since she's a clone, and she's been connected to the system for the duration of her existence, she knew of the device and, best we can tell, figured out how to disable it."

"So, you have no idea where she is? There's no footage of her leaving?" Xander shook his head in disbelief.

"Once she left the complex, we lost track of her. Last we saw of her," Trevor bent over the map on the table and pointed, "she was going this way. Gavin, of course, has security out looking for her, but if she did disable her tracker, it'll be difficult to find her."

Xander looked where Trevor had indicated and swallowed hard. R3 was heading in the direction of Fertile Lake. He ran a hand through his hair as he paced the room. He couldn't stay here, that much was obvious. If R3 made it to the lake and Sabine wasn't there to help her… He stopped short. "Trevor, where's Sabine? Did she make it here? Is she still here?"

"She was, but Gavin let her leave. Escorted her out himself yesterday morn—"

"*Let* her leave? What do you mean?"

Trevor glanced around the room, then back at Xander. "Gavin locked her up after she was treated for the scorpion sting."

"Oh God." Xander leaned forward with his elbows resting on his knees. "You better start at the beginning and tell me everything."

Fifteen

Sabine walked through the night. At first, every step was cautious, careful, lest she trip over something and make a bad situation worse. After a while, her confidence grew. The ground was flat, dry, and barren. Nothing grew here, nothing was left here but dead earth stretching endlessly into the night. Simply put, there was nothing to trip over, so she trudged along until the darkness eased and the pale outlines of mountains in the distance became visible.

She stopped and retrieved her canteen, wincing in pain as tears spilled down her cheeks to mix with the water as she drank. The enormous boulders that hid the cave's entrance were within sight. She was going to make it.

A fragment of another memory flashed through her mind; her mother's voice scolding her for a long-forgotten bit of mischief. *"I give you an inch and you take a country mile."* She'd always wondered how far a country mile was, and now, looking at the boulders, she finally had an idea and was about to walk three of them. Near as she could figure, anyway.

Smiling, she set out again, the pain in her arm fading into the background along with the memory.

ა ა ა

Xander leaned back in his chair, mind reeling. "Are you sure that's what you want me to do?"

Standing with his arms crossed, Trevor's lips tightened in a grim line. "It's the only chance they've got."

"How many did you say there are?" Xander couldn't believe he was contemplating this insane request, but he might as well get all the facts.

"There are forty-two old enough to travel."

"Forty-two," he muttered. Forty-two lives he'd be responsible for—forty-two *children*. What Trevor was asking seemed impossible. It was a two-day trek by himself. How much longer with children in tow? "How am I supposed to carry enough food and water for them all?"

Trevor nodded at Xander's pack. "They'll each carry their own."

"And how the hell do you propose to get us out of here unseen?"

"Does that mean you'll do it?"

Xander stood and paced the room yet again, his thoughts on Aria, Felicity, and Neriah. The three of them each carried a fertilized embryo that would trigger an active pregnancy at a specific time. Thanks to Sabine getting them to the lake, those girls would have live births.

It was hard to think of them as clones. Not just hard—impossible. They each had individual personalities, likes, and dislikes. They laughed and played like children, had their own thoughts and ideas.

It all came down to one thing, he realized. Due to circumstances far beyond their control, these second-gen clones were on a path that led to an early demise. They deserved to live.

"I'll do it," he said, shocked by his own audacity even as he spoke. "I'll take them to the lake. But you damn well better have a plan to get us out of here safely."

Looking both relieved and excited, Trevor clapped Xander on the shoulder and steered him toward the bank of computers. "I've got the mother of all plans."

ૐ ૐ ૐ

She'd made it. Sabine stumbled the last few steps to the boulder, then collapsed against it, her breath coming in ragged, heaving gulps. She ripped the mask from her face, letting it fall in the dirt at her feet. Her shoulders shook with unsuppressed sobs as she rested her cheek on the heated rock. A wave of lightheadedness swept over her, and she nearly crumpled to the ground, only the solid mass of rock holding her upright.

She took several deep, steadying breaths, then wiped the tears from her face. She'd fucking made it. Now, all she had to do was get to Dalton's and he'd take care of the rest.

Pushing off from the boulder, she took the first step. "One foot in front of the other," she murmured, taking another step. A few moments later, she was inside the tunnels, the cooler air a relief to her tortured body.

With no flashlight, she used the jagged stone walls to feel her way through the darkness, fighting rising nausea every step of the way. As she got closer, sounds of life reached her ears. Muffled voices, thuds and clangs, a goat bleating.

Almost there…

She staggered toward the cavern, crumpling to the ground the moment she stepped into the light. Everything around her faded to black, the word

"Dalton!" echoing in the far recesses of her mind.

"You sure this'll work?" Xander asked, staring at the monitor in front of him. Forty-two young clone girls sat in a classroom, their attention focused on the woman at the front of the room. "Do they even know they're going anywhere?"

"They don't know yet," Trevor said. "I doubt they could all keep that a secret. When the time comes, we'll escort them to the decontamination room, outfit them with masks and backpacks, and tell them they're going on a field trip." He nudged Xander on the shoulder. "And yes, it'll work."

"How long did you say the cameras will be down for?" Xander's gaze went to the alternating views on the security monitors. A regular flow of people moved through the hallways, going in and out of doors, and stopping to chat at times. He had his doubts they could maintain a loop for long enough, undetected.

"Thirty minutes, and you don't need to worry about that. I've got people on the inside all over this place," Trevor replied. "The plan is to get you and the girls out of here tomorrow, if everything is ready, and if not, then the day after."

"And until then?" Xander asked.

"Until then, you eat and rest." Trevor motioned to a

door in the far corner of the room. "There's a bunk where you can sleep, and a shower. I'm having some food brought down for you, but it'll be about an hour."

Getting to his feet, Xander nodded, then grabbed his pack and crossed the room. Right now, a shower sounded like a great idea.

ʒ ʒ ʒ

Hours later, Xander was startled awake by a banging on the door. Forgetting where he was, he sat up fast and smacked his head on the top bunk frame. "What the f—"

"Get up!" The door crashed open, and a light flicked on.

Xander scowled at the intrusion and rubbed his head. "What the hell is going on?"

"Gavin and half the security force are gone," Trevor snapped. "We're doing this now, so get your ass up!"

"Gone? Where?" Xander scrambled to his feet and followed Trevor.

"According to my sources, they've gone after Sabine," he said, his voice tight.

Xander let loose a string of curse words as he glared at Trevor. "That'll lead them right to the lake. I can't take those kids there now."

"You can and you will," Trevor said, his voice grim. "I'm taking a team and going out to stop Gavin.

136

Your job is to get those kids to safety. My job is to worry about Gavin." They entered the main room, and Trevor looked around. "Where we at, people?"

The room was buzzing with activity. Four people at the bank of computers were furiously typing and talking amongst themselves. Three more sporting security patches were suiting up to go outside, while a few others were taking stock of weapons piled on the table.

Trevor went to the wall of computers and bent to look at a monitor. "How long until the girls are ready to go?"

"We're getting them ready now. It takes a while to suit forty-two kids, but I've got a team working on it."

Xander found the stack of outdoor gear and, opening his backpack, started filling it with supplies. "Is there a first-aid kit around here?"

"Over there." A security guard pointed to the far corner by the ladder.

"Thanks, man." Xander hesitated a moment. "I worked security here not long ago. I've never seen any of you before."

"That's because we don't work for security. We're with The Opposition." With no further explanation, the man nodded to Xander's backpack. "You best get your shit together. We'll be leaving soon."

Just then, Trevor called out, "Get ready people. We move in ten."

ꝫ ꝫ ꝫ

Xander peered in the window of the decontamination chamber, where forty-two little girls stood lined up, putting masks on. He turned to Trevor. "So, we're just gonna waltz right out of here like nothing is happening?"

"Thirty-minute loop, remember?" Trevor tapped his earpiece and grinned. "We've got eyes down below. They'll let us know which way to go. We won't be seen."

"And the girls, they'll listen to us?" Xander glanced at the children again, thinking about Neriah and how excited she got over everything. It was going to be a job keeping these kids muted long enough to get out of here.

"They've been told they're taking a field trip to see the desert and they need to be quiet inside the building so they don't disturb those who are working." Trevor clapped him on the shoulder. "They'll listen."

Nodding, Xander took a step back. "We going in?"

"After you." Trevor motioned to the door.

Xander turned the knob and went inside, Trevor right behind him.

It was eerily quiet in the decontamination chamber, as not one of the children made a sound at their arrival. Instead, they stood silently, masks in place, backpacks on.

"Girls, this is Xander and Trevor," a woman in front of the room said, pointing to both men in turn. "They're going to be taking you into the desert, so you need to listen to every single thing they tell you to do."

Trevor stepped forward. "Thanks, Greta." He pivoted to face the girls. "Raise your hand if you're ready to go."

In unison, forty-two hands went up in an instant.

Xander smiled. This might actually work.

"Remember, we're not going to make a peep until we get outside the gates. There are a lot of people working on important things here and we don't want to bother them, or they may not let us take any more field trips." Trevor paused as he looked around. "Understand?"

Forty-two small albino heads bobbed in response.

Trevor glanced over his shoulder at Xander and jerked his head, indicating he should come forward.

Xander moved to stand next to Trevor. "Stay with us, stay in line, and no wandering."

Turning, Trevor went to the door, then poked his head outside before glancing at Xander with a nod. "Let's go."

Greta held the door as they all filed out of the room, with Trevor leading the way. Xander waited until the last girl left, then hurried to catch up with Trevor as the rest of the guards on their team fell in behind the procession.

With only the sound of footsteps echoing in the empty hallways, they made their way to the side door leading to the greenhouses. Once there, Trevor paused, holding his fingers over the device in his ear as he listened for a moment. With a terse nod, he opened the door.

Xander stood by the doorway, double-checking that each girl still had her mask in place as they went through. Satisfied, he once again caught up to Trevor as they wound their way between the greenhouses.

Before long, they were at the edge of the desert, only the fence between them and freedom. Trevor stepped up to the gate without hesitation and punched in a code. The gate swung open, and they silently filed through.

Trevor kept his fingers over the device in his ear, while Xander kept glancing back. Once the fence was out of sight, they finally stopped.

"You girls did a great job of staying quiet," Trevor said. "Come, gather around. Let's talk about today's outing."

Excited murmuring filled the air as the girls broke from their line and clumped together in groups of friends, filling all the space around Xander and Trevor.

"First, I have a surprise for all of you," Trevor announced. "This isn't just a field trip for a day. It's an overnight trip!"

The murmurs rose to a loud chatter, and some of the children jumped up and down.

Despite the dire situation, Xander couldn't help but smile at their enthusiasm. Perhaps this wasn't going to be as difficult as he'd first thought. At least, as far as getting the girls to cooperate and behave. They seemed amiable enough.

Trevor nudged Xander with his elbow and leaned close. "Don't tell them about the lake, just in case we all get caught. We'll stick with cave exploring for now."

Nodding, Xander took over the announcement. "We're going to a special cave I know of to do some exploring. How's that for exciting?"

The volume of chattering raised again, this time to squeals of delight.

He waited until the kids had settled enough for him to be heard. "It's a two-day walk, so it's important you all follow some rules."

Xander stood in front of the forty-two little masked faces and, as they listened with rapt attention, gave them the rules.

Sixteen

A murky voice sounded in the distance. Fire scorched Sabine's arm. Her cheek pressed against something gritty. She tried to move, but the ground swayed beneath her. Nausea rose and burst from her mouth before she could stop it.

Acrid vomit filled her nostrils and a warm pool of stink spread around her face. She grasped a handful of dirt and tried again to move, pushing herself up with all her might. Her injured arm failed her, and she collapsed back into the puddle of puke.

From the far recesses of her mind, she heard a familiar voice.

"Get her to my place…"

Dalton.

She surrendered to the gathering darkness.

ᘐ ᘐ ᘐ

"Excuse me, please, Xander?" One of the girls stepped forward and squared her shoulders.

Smiling at the brave gesture, he asked, "What's your name?"

"Zuri," she said, lifting her chin a fraction.

"Do you have a question for me, Zuri?"

"I'm the oldest and I can help you with the younger ones."

He was impressed, not only by her offer, but by her courage. "What do you have in mind?"

"We sing sometimes in class, recite poetry, read out loud to each other. Maybe we can do some things like that while we walk." Zuri glanced around at her sisters. "It'll keep us all occupied."

"That's a great idea," he agreed. "Why don't you pick a song to get us started? We'll be leaving in a minute. I just need to talk to Trevor first."

Clasping her hands together, Zuri skipped away to join the others as Xander turned to Trevor. "What route do you want us to go?"

"My scouts tell me they've tracked Gavin's group to the rim of Devil's Canyon. Looks like they're walking the edge," Trevor said.

Xander frowned. "That's the long way. If they're following Sabine, maybe she knew someone was behind her and went that way hoping to lose them."

"Maybe. I don't know about her tracks, only Gavin's group. So, that's the way we're going." Trevor gestured ahead of them. "You take the girls straight through and into the Joshua Tree Forest, the same route you took when you went before. We'll skirt around the rim of the canyon double-time. We'll cut them off before they get there."

Nodding, Xander glanced at the girls again, the weight of his responsibility settling on his shoulders. "I'll approach with caution once we get close, just in case."

"Sounds good, man." Trevor held out his hand for a brief handshake. "Be safe out there."

"You too." Xander watched him and his men leave, then turned to the girls. "Who's ready to go?"

ॐ ॐ ॐ

Several hours and more songs than he could count later, Xander and his flock of kids reached their first rest spot; a huge mound of dirt known as "The Humpback". It'd been his first landmark on his own journey and was about halfway to the forest's edge.

Stopping by the base of the hill, he removed his pack. "Let's take a rest, girls. Does everyone remember how to make a dome shelter over your heads using your jackets?"

A rising chorus of "yeses" rose as he pulled out a ration bar and a canteen.

"Good, now each of you get a bar and your canteen. That's your snack. Even if you're not hungry or thirsty, I want you to eat and drink. You need the energy." He put his bar in his pocket and strapped the canteen around his wrist, then waited as the group did the same (one of the rules he'd set forth; follow all directions to the letter). "All right, everyone sit and dome up."

Xander waited as all forty-two girls did as instructed before making his own little jacket dome. He tore into his ration bar, devouring it in four bites, then drank some water. Quickly putting his mask back on, he then removed his dome and watched over the children.

When they were finished with their snack, each one raised a hand (another rule of his) and waited. Once all forty-two hands were up, he called out, "Masks back on, then domes off."

Impressed again, Xander relaxed a bit. They were going to be fine.

꒐ ꒐ ꒐

Sabine opened her eyes and looked around. Blurry images of four walls, a door, a ceiling; a tiny room, greeted her. She blinked a few times, trying to clear her vision. Pushing herself up in bed, she reached for the cup on the side table to relieve her cotton-mouth and realized the fiery pain in her arm had been reduced to a minor ache.

Dalton's... She was at Dalton's.

She drank deep, knowing it was lake water, then sighed. In the next room, she heard dishes clattering, and a moment later, a knock, then voices.

Words were exchanged, and the voices rose in volume, though she still couldn't make out what was being said.

She got to her feet, placing her palm against the wall for support, and steadied herself. It was time to go see what was going on out there. With cautious steps, she made her way to the door and opened it.

Four heads turned in her direction. Dalton and the council members.

By nightfall, Xander and his group had reached the edge of the Joshua Tree Forest. Keeping in mind the story Trevor had told him about Sabine's scorpion sting, he thoroughly checked the chosen campsite before telling the girls to settle in.

Leaving Zuri in charge, he went and gathered enough dead wood for the night, then built a fire. They didn't need it for cooking, but the girls took advantage and told stories. When instructed, they all domed up and chowed down on freeze-dried fruit and ration bars.

Not long after that, the girls were all sleeping and Xander lay looking at the black sky, wondering if Trevor had caught up to Gavin. If not, he'd need a plan for getting away unseen.

Surely Gavin and his men would leave tracks going into the cave if they'd made it. He'd have to keep a close eye out once the boulders were in sight. There was only one way in and out, so if anyone had come or gone recently, he'd know.

Unless they covered their steps. It would be the smart thing to do.

Hell, he'd done it himself, until his mind had succumbed to the delusions from exposure.

Still, he'd watch for signs.

A sudden thought occurred to him that made his stomach churn. He and the girls were leaving a trail akin to stampeding cattle. If Gavin wasn't stopped, and was somehow behind them, they'd be leading him right to the cave.

He had to start covering the evidence of their journey.

Turning to his side, his mind raced, trying to come up with a solution.

By morning, Xander had an idea. He and a few of the older girls gathered long spiny branches from the dead Joshua trees, while Zuri kept an eye on the rest of the group. When they returned, each girl old enough to bear the extra weight and bulk was outfitted with a branch on either side of their backpack, secured with the canteen clips, and left to drag behind them. The younger girls who couldn't drag branches each got an extra canteen clipped to their packs.

It wasn't a perfect solution, but it was all he had.

The going was slow, the air hot, and by the time they stopped for their first break, everyone was drenched in sweat.

After a respite of only fifteen minutes, they were back to trudging through the dead forest.

Xander was impressed. These girls were real troopers, and if they got there safe, he resolved to make it a personal responsibility to watch over each and every one of them.

Sabine stepped into the main room and nodded at Dalton and the council members as she made her way to the table. "Ellen, Warren, Matthew. You'll forgive me if I need to sit. I've had a rough few days—weeks, actually."

"That's why we're here," Ellen said, sitting across

from her. "What happened to you?"

Sabine filled them in on everything, then glanced at Dalton. "Where are the girls? Are they well?"

"They're just fine," he assured her. "I sent them to The Square for rations. They should be back soon." He hesitated a moment, then asked, "You're not really returning them to RaShell, are you?"

"I don't have a choice," she said, looking at each of them in turn. "The world is dying up there and I can do something to save it. But I need the lab, I need the resources—"

"You need to keep those girls safe!" Dalton's tone filled with anger. "You made a promise to them, to me, to all of us here."

"I'm not going back on that promise," she argued. "You don't really think Gavin would hurt them, do you?"

"No, but he'd damn well hurt you, and you know it! How do you propose to keep any of your promises if you're locked up or dead?"

Sabine opened her mouth to protest, but Matthew stopped her with a look.

"That's enough now. No one is going anywhere until we hear your plan." He gave her a pointed stare. "Every detail."

"We all have a duty to these girls now," Warren added. "We must be assured of their safety as well as that of their future children."

"That is why you brought them here, after all." Ellen reached across and patted Sabine's hand. "You said you wanted to use Fertile Lake to ensure the health of both them and their unborn children to come. Well, now they've drunk from the lake, and their well-being is in our hands as well as yours."

The three men murmured their agreement.

Sabine took a deep breath, hoping she could make them understand. "If there was a way for me to conduct my research here, a proper lab with the technology I need to replicate the lake water…well, things would be different. But there's not. We don't have those things here and I need them. What would you have me do?"

"Give me some time," Dalton said. "I'm sure I can rig something up—"

"I need more than a rigged-up lab. I know you know that." She stood and went to Dalton, pleading for his support. "I don't have a choice. I've got to take the girls—"

"We won't go."

Sabine turned to find Aria standing in the doorway. "Oh, sweetie—"

"No." Aria's gaze swept the room, then landed back on Sabine. "We're not going back, and you can't make us."

Seventeen

ater the next day, the boulders that hid the cave's entrance came into sight. Xander looked around one last time to be sure he saw nothing but endless, flat, empty land, then turned to the girls. "Line up behind me and stay quiet. It's going to be dark in the tunnel, so we'll use the cave wall to guide us. Raise your hand when you're ready to go."

After a bit of shuffling, the girls were lined up with their hands raised.

With one last look at the desert to confirm they were alone, Xander led them to the boulders. Walking in the meager shade, he followed the path to the cave. He stopped at the opening and motioned to Zuri. "Wait here and make sure all the girls are accounted for. Have them take off their masks as they enter, then bring up the rear."

Nodding, she positioned herself at the side of the entrance.

He took a deep breath, removed his own mask, then stepped into the darkness.

They walked for a while and as they got deeper into the tunnel, faint voices drifted through the air.

Xander smiled. They'd made it. Sabine would be proud. He hoped like hell she was here.

Ahead, the voices got louder, and he realized something wasn't right.

He stopped moving and was bumped from behind by one of the girls.

"Eeep! Sorry." Her soft voice echoed through the tunnel.

"Shh," he admonished, trying to figure out what he was hearing. It sounded like…arguing. And it sounded angry.

Startled cries of, "Oops, sorry, and ouch," filled the tunnel as the line came to an unexpected halt.

Shit! There was no hiding the noise, so he figured they might as well press on. He hadn't got more than a few steps further when a few words bellowed through the tunnel and stopped him cold.

"Where are my girls?"

Gavin.

Xander turned and waited for the girl behind him to catch up. Putting his hand on her head, he leaned down and whispered. "Stay here, don't move." He worked his way down the line, telling each girl the same thing. When he reached the end, he put his hand atop the last head. "Zuri?"

"Yes," she said softly.

"Something is wrong, and I need to go see what it is. You keep the girls here until I either come back or send someone for you."

He felt her nod, then let go of her head and took her by the hand, leading her to the front of the line. Once there, he patted her shoulder, then crept forward, toward the arguing.

How the hell did Gavin get here? There were no tracks. And where the hell is Trevor?

It didn't matter. He was here and now there was nothing to do but deal with it.

"Gavin, please. If you'll let me show you—"
Sabine!

"—thing I want to see are my girls. Now!"

The dim light ahead got brighter with each step until Xander reached the mouth of the tunnel. He crouched in the shadows and surveyed the scene before him.

They weren't as close as he'd first thought, the cave just had an echo that carried. Gavin and five guards were standing in a circle around Sabine, off to the left at the head of the trail leading to her campsite. Dalton's was to the right, out of the line-of-sight.

With a glance over his shoulder to be sure there were no white-haired girls to be seen, he bent forward, keeping his head low, and made a dash for Dalton's.

He didn't bother to knock once he got there, just opened the door and slipped inside. A quick look around told him Dalton wasn't there. He peeked out the small window and saw the man hunched behind his old truck bed trailer, watching something off to his left.

Xander cracked the door open and, after confirming there was no one in sight but Dalton, scurried out to join him. He placed a hand on the man's shoulder and, when he jumped, pressed a finger to his lips.

Dalton nodded and gestured to his hut.

With a quick bob of his head, Xander followed Dalton inside. "What the hell is going on?" he asked in a loud whisper.

"Sabine came back a couple of days ago, hurt and delirious. I treated her myself, made sure she recovered. She was just on her way to go check on the girls when Gavin and his assholes showed up."

"So, he hasn't seen the girls yet?"

"Not yet." Dalton's lips pressed into a thin line. "But it's only a matter of time."

"Is there any other way to get to them?"

"There's a path to the right. It's clear from what I can tell, but you have to cut across the lake's shore and through The Square. Do you think you could make it there? I can keep watch here, distract them if needed."

Xander nodded, then sighed. "I need to tell you something."

There must've been something about the tone of his voice, because Dalton gave him a sharp look. "What is it?"

"I didn't come here alone."

Dalton's eyes narrowed. "What do you mean?"

"Trevor assigned me as guardian over forty-two second-gen clones and tasked me with getting them here—"

"What?" Dalton's eyebrows shot high on his forehead. "Where are they?"

"I left them in the tunnel when I heard voices and realized it was Gavin." Xander ran a hand through his hair. "Think I can take them with me on that route to Sabine's?"

"Not through The Square, that'll bring too much attention." Dalton looked away, his jaw clenched as he peered out the window.

"Well, I can't just leave them there."

"No. No, you can't." Dalton glanced around the small hut, then returned his gaze to Xander. "You'll have to bring them here."

"Here?" It was Xander's turn to survey the two-room hut now. "You think they'll all fit?"

"Fuck if I know. Maybe?" Dalton paced the room, pointing. "We can probably get half of them in the bedroom, and the rest in here. It'll be tight, and only until we figure out what the hell to do—goddamn Trevor, anyway—but we're short on options."

Xander went to the window again. "Looks like the coast is still clear."

"You better go now, get them all in one trip. I'll go keep watch out by the trailer. If I see Gavin head this way, I'll go cause a distraction."

Reaching for the doorknob, Xander paused a second. "Be careful."

"You too."

ʒ ʒ ʒ

Sabine folded her arms and glared at Gavin. "I can't do that, not yet. I'm sorry." Her mind was racing, trying to figure out how he'd tracked her. She'd checked her pack, her clothing—she hadn't found anything.

"And why not?" Gavin took a step toward her. "The secret is out now. We know where the lake is, where all these people have been hiding. It's time for them to come home."

She stepped back, keeping the distance between them. Unsure if he was referring to the colonists of the lake or the girls, she realized it didn't matter. "They are home."

"You're being unreasonable." Gavin moved forward again.

She backed up. "*I'm* being unreasonable? How did you find me? This place?"

Gavin gave her a sly grin. "You didn't check your food."

"You put a tracking device in my food?" She heard the astonishment in her voice and shook her head. "How did I not notice?"

A brief cackle escaped Gavin. "You think all tracking devices are little pieces of metal or plastic? How quaint." He casually strolled forward. "Come now, let me see the girls."

Sabine moved back several steps. She had to do something. At this rate, she'd be walking them right to her camp. Her best hope at that point would be for Aria to take her sisters and circle round to Dalton's place, which she'd instructed the girl to do if she heard any voices other than Sabine's. She motioned in the direction of the lake. "Gavin, please. If you'll just let me show you—"

"The only thing I want to see are my girls," he barked. Reaching into his waistband, he drew a gun and pointed it at her. "Now!"

Eighteen

Xander made his way back to the tunnel. Though it was totally dark, he felt their presence as sure as he felt his own. "Zuri," he whispered into the inky blackness.

"Right here," she whispered back.

Following her voice, he carefully inched forward until her outstretched hand touched his arm. He clasped her hand in his own and squeezed. "Hold hands and be quiet. Pass it on," he said, his whisper so faint he barely heard it himself.

Zuri squeezed his hand back.

He felt her arm pull tight as she presumably leaned toward the next in line.

A few moments later, Zuri squeezed his hand one

more time. "We're ready."

Leading the way, Xander moved toward the cavern. As soon as there was enough dim light to see, he turned and confirmed the girls were behind him, all holding hands, the line stretching into the darkness.

His lips twitched in a brief pleased smile. These kids were amazing, the way they followed directions to the letter. As they approached the mouth of the tunnel, the arguing voices echoed louder than before.

Whatever was happening was escalating.

He paused in the opening, spared a quick glance around, and saw only two of the guards off to the left now. But Gavin's voice could be heard coming from that direction, so Xander flashed his gaze to where Dalton was hiding behind his trailer.

The man waved them forward and Xander bent low and tugged on Zuri's hand. A brief look over his shoulder confirmed she, along with the others, were all crouched over.

Xander tightened his grip on Zuri's hand and hurried across the open stretch to Dalton's.

The door was open and ready.

He counted heads as the girls ran inside, the only noise, muffled footsteps in the dirt.

Forty-two...thank God!

Xander went in behind them, then Dalton, who shut the door with a soft 'click'.

Zuri rushed forward, wrapping her arms around Xander's waist and hugging him tight. "Thank you."

Patting her back, he looked around at the crowded room. Some of the girls had shuffled into the bedroom already, as there wasn't enough space to fit them all in the main room.

"I need you all to stay quiet," Xander said, keeping his voice as low as he could. "Aria, Felicity, and Neriah are out there, and I need to go get them. This is Dalton, and he's going to keep you safe while I'm gone."

"You're coming back, though, right?" Zuri asked, looking up at him.

He smiled at her. "I'm coming back. Now, get your sisters settled. You can each eat your last ration bar and have some water while I'm gone, but please, no talking."

Zuri squared her small shoulders and took charge.

Dalton clapped Xander on the shoulder. "Good man," he said softly. "You best get going."

With a brief bob of his head, Xander slipped from the hut, darting to the path on the right.

ᘓ ᘓ ᘓ

Sabine froze. "Gavin?"

"I mean it," he growled. "I want my girls and you're going to take me to them. No more excuses, no more delays. Now move!"

She was out of ideas. For her own sake, as well as

everyone else here, she had to do as he said. Her only consolation was she knew Gavin would never hurt the girls. As for herself, she wouldn't have thought so, but as she stood looking at the gun pointed at her, she realized she was wrong. He would kill her to get them back.

"Okay, Gavin, you win. I'll take you to them." She jerked her head to the trail behind her. "This way."

"After you," he said, holding the gun steady. "And if you try anything, I'll shoot."

The last of her hopes were dashed when she glanced at the guards and saw them, hands on their weapons at their waists, ready to draw.

Turning, she started toward her camp.

 махмахмах

Xander ran down the trail, heedless of the uneven ground, of the curious onlookers as he passed huts, and then the sandy beach. He kept running when he got to The Square, skirting the outer edge behind the booths, and shoving a few people out of his way.

When he reached Sabine's camp, he heard voices on the other trail, and knew he was almost out of time. Heart racing, his gaze darted around the campsite, finally landing on the three girls huddled inside the medical tent under the exam table.

Waving them over to him, he gave them a quick

hug, then ushered them out of sight behind a cluster of nearby boulders.

Just as they ducked down, Sabine's voice called out, "Aria, Felicity, Neriah… I'm back."

Neriah perked up, but Xander put a hand on her arm and shook his head.

Embracing the younger girl, Aria met Xander's gaze.

He lifted a finger to his lips and the three girls nodded.

"Where are they?" Gavin's voice rang out, his anger evident.

"I left them here, I swear! I don't know where they went. Maybe they're hiding?" A short pause, and then, "That gun is going to scare them. Why don't you put it away?"

"Shut up," Gavin growled. "I'll do no such thing until I get them back. Where. Are. They?"

"Help me look," Sabine said, her voice shaky. "There are plenty of places to hide around here."

"You two, check the shacks, and you two, check around the campsite," Gavin ordered.

Xander pointed the way he'd come, then put up one finger, then two, then three. Snatching Neriah into his arms, he bent as low as he could with the child and ran. He glanced over his shoulder to find Aria and Felicity right behind him.

When they got close to The Square, he asked Aria, "What's the quickest way around?"

She pointed to a few huts on the edge, and they changed direction to run behind them.

They slowed the pace as they darted from building to building, keeping to the shadows and out of sight. When they reached the beach, there was nowhere to hide, so Xander let Aria and Felicity go in front of him and they simply ran. With every step, he half-expected a bullet to the back, but none came.

Once they reached the trailhead, he risked a look behind him. Luck was with them; no one followed. As he caught his breath, an idea came to him. A way to stop Gavin, to prove to him Fertile Lake was the future.

He stopped running. "Aria!"

Coming to an abrupt halt, she turned, eyebrows scrunched in question.

"Take your sisters to Dalton's. You're almost there, you'll make it."

"But…where are you going?"

"To get Marina."

༄ ༄ ༄

"What is the meaning of this?"

Sabine's head snapped up as Ellen, Matthew, and Warren entered her camp.

"Don't make me repeat myself," Warren said,

glaring at Gavin.

"I've come for my girls," Gavin answered. He waved the gun at Sabine. "She kidnapped them and I demand she give them back."

"That's a serious accusation," Ellen said, her gaze never leaving Gavin. "How about you put that gun down and we'll talk?"

Giving a harsh laugh, Gavin shook his head. "We're way past that, I'm afraid."

Taking a step closer, Matthew held out his hand. "Come now, let's not be unreasonable. Give me the gun."

Gavin fired.

Matthew crumpled to the ground, a bright red blossom spreading across his chest.

Ellen screamed.

The guards came running, weapons drawn.

Gasping, Sabine dropped to her knees next to Matthew and felt for a pulse. Weak, thready, then...gone. "He's dead," she whispered.

Warren moved by in a blur, and another shot rang out.

Before Sabine could register what was happening, one more shot exploded. Both Warren and Ellen lay bleeding in the dirt.

"What did you do?" Sabine bellowed, scrambling to check on Warren.

He lay on his back, blood gurgling from his mouth. His terror-filled eyes were wide as he reached a hand out.

Gavin grabbed Sabine by the hair and yanked her away. "Leave him! He's gone. They're all dead." He pressed his gun to her temple. "Where are my girls?"

She took a deep, steadying breath. "If you kill me, you'll never find them."

Nineteen

Xander heard the gunshots in time to duck behind the boulder near Sabine's camp. Crawling, he peeked around the corner to see the council members lying dead in the dirt and Gavin with a gun to Sabine's head.

Words were exchanged, though he couldn't make them out. Gavin grabbed Sabine by the arm and jerked her to her feet. Keeping the gun pointed to the back of her head, he marched her out of camp and down the path leading to The Square, his guards following after.

Xander hesitated, his frantic glance going between the path to Marina's and the path Sabine was on. If he went after Sabine, what could he do? He had no gun, no way to take out Gavin *and* five guards. But if he got to

Marina, and quick, her pregnancy could be the key to deescalating the hostage situation.

Marina.

Decision made, he took off at a dead run.

Sabine stumbled along the path, her mind racing as ideas were discarded as quickly as they came. She couldn't let him take her to The Square, she knew that much. There were too many innocent people there and, as he'd demonstrated, he wouldn't hesitate to use them against her.

There was only one person who might be able to help her.

Dalton.

She came to an abrupt halt and raised her hands in defeat. "I give up, Gavin. I'll take you to them."

He spun her around and placed the barrel of the gun against her forehead. Staring, he searched her eyes for a moment, then pulled the gun back a few inches. "If you're lying, I will gather every traitor down here and make them watch while I torture you. I'll shoot both of your kneecaps, then both elbows. After that, I'll bury you up to your neck and set your hair on fire. When I'm done with you, you'll beg me to kill you, but I won't. I'll let you suffer. Understood?"

Sabine swallowed hard and nodded. She pointed to

a path leading away from The Square and toward Dalton's. "This way."

ᘐ ᘐ ᘐ

Xander reached the campsite and skidded to a halt in front of a visibly pregnant woman he didn't recognize. "Marina," he gasped.

The woman frowned and didn't answer.

Grabbing her by the shoulders, he shook her. "Where is she?"

She jerked away and pointed to the communal fire pit. "Over there."

Without so much as a thank you, he took off. "Marina," he yelled as he got close.

Marina turned, long wooden spoon in hand. "What're you—what's wrong?"

"No time to explain, just come with me," he panted, reaching for her hand.

She backed away from him. "I'm not going with you until I know what the hell is going on."

"Please, it's the girls. I'll explain on the way, I promise."

"You'll explain now or I'm not going." She planted a hand on her hip and tapped her foot.

Frustrated, he slapped his hand against his thigh. "Gavin has come from RaShell. He wants the girls and is killing people to get them."

"So, give them back."

"We can't give them back. The pregnant clones are dying. We brought them here to see if Fertile Lake could fix the problem."

"And how is seeing me going to help the situation?"

"If he sees you, a pregnant woman, sees it's possible to reproduce, he'll believe Sabine about the lake being the key. Now, please…I need your help." He knew hadn't told her even close to all of the truth, because there was simply no time.

After a slight hesitation, she nodded, then turned to another pregnant woman. "Cara, leave one person here in charge of the little ones, then gather the rest of the women and children and meet us at…" she glanced at Xander with a lifted eyebrow.

"Dalton's," he supplied, unsure of a more secure meeting place than that.

"Meet us at Dalton's. Come as quickly as possible." Marina dropped the spoon on a flat rock by the firepit, then nodded at him. "If one preggo will give him something to consider, imagine when he sees all of us, and the children."

Xander held out a hand to her. "Ready?"

Sabine walked slowly, feigning a limp. She knew Dalton would do what he could to convince Gavin to give her research a chance, but the man was clearly unstable. And he didn't seem interested in listening anymore. She just hoped the girls had stayed hidden, wherever they were.

They came to a break in the trail, the left side going straight to Dalton's, while the other side veered off to the right, passing between a cluster of huts and the lake. She hesitated only a second before choosing the long way to Dalton's. She needed to buy as much time as she could.

ვ ვ ვ

The going was careful with a pregnant woman in tow, and Xander had to force himself to slow down so she could keep up. When they finally reached the trail leading to The Square, he paused a moment to let her rest. Other than the panting from Marina, it was quiet. Too quiet.

"Wait right here, I'm just going to go have a look and see if Gavin is in The Square."

He patted her hand, and she waved him away.

"Look, if they come back this way—"

"I know how to hide," she glanced down and rubbed a hand over her belly, "despite this massive thing. Go, and hurry back."

Xander smiled and turned, taking off at a jog down the trail. As he approached The Square, he stopped, straining as he listened for anything out of the ordinary.

Nothing unusual. Just the normal sounds of people bustling to and fro. He crept closer, a few vendor's voices sounding above the crowds.

Surely, they'd heard the gunshots—Sabine's campsite wasn't that far from here. Yet they were still carrying on as usual? He didn't get it. After a quick look around, and seeing he was still alone, he hurried to the nearest booth.

Iver, the man selling ribbons, scowled at him. "Where's those kids? Off destroying someone else's wares?"

Ignoring the question, Xander asked one of his own. "Have you heard anything unusual today?"

"Like what?"

"Loud pops, three of them."

"Oh yeah, a while ago. Figured it was Sabine doing them experiments again or something."

"What experiments?"

Iver frowned. "Now look here, I don't know what she does up there, and I don't much care, long as she keeps them kids with her and outta my hair. But she did something a while back, made some loud noises and got herself a good talking to from the council. She hasn't done it since, until today."

Xander ran a hand through his hair and turned to look around. Everything seemed fine here, business as usual. Gavin wasn't here and hadn't been at all, from what he could tell.

"That it?" Iver asked, his voice grumpier than before. "I got customers waiting."

"Yeah, thanks." Xander moved out of the way as a woman nodded to him and stepped up to the booth.

With no idea where to even look now, he headed back up the trail.

ༀ ༀ ༀ

Sabine was out of time. As she approached Dalton's, her stomach twisted in knots.

"Whose place is this?" Gavin demanded, grabbing her arm and bringing her to a halt.

"Dalton's."

"Dalton? Holy fuck, you don't mean..." Gavin released her and waved his gun at the hut. "He was the second one to up and disappear while working for me. Hey Dalton! Get out here!"

Please don't let the girls be here...

The door cracked open and Dalton peeked out. "Gavin? What're you doing here? What's with the gun?"

"Come join the party." Gavin motioned to him.

After a slight hesitation, Dalton slipped outside, shutting the door behind him. He eyed the guards, then Sabine, before returning his gaze to Gavin. "What's going on?"

"I came to get my girls." He leaned to the side, trying to look behind Dalton. "They in there? Aria! Felicity...Neriah!"

Silence filled the air.

Sabine saw Dalton's finger twitch, and she met his gaze. Eyebrows slightly scrunched, he gave the tiniest nod possible, and her heart sank. They were here.

"Girls! Come out now, it's time to go home!"

Gavin made a move to go to the door, but Dalton sidestepped, stopping him. "They're scared," he said, giving the gun a pointed look. "Let me go get them."

Pressing the gun to Sabine's temple, Gavin said, "You've got one minute, then she dies."

ॐ ॐ ॐ

Xander and Marina got to Dalton's in time to see him come out his front door with Aria, Felicity, and Neriah in tow. Five guards surrounded Sabine, while Gavin stood with his gun pointed at her head.

Tightening his grip on Marina's hand, he pulled her forward. "Wait! Gavin—wait!"

Everyone turned as he and Marina came rushing into the yard.

Mouth hanging open, Gavin stared at Marina and her huge pregnant belly.

"Just wait," Xander panted. "Look, Sabine was

right. Fertile Lake is the answer."

"It's a f-f-fluke." Gavin gawked at the evidence before him. He reached out, as if to touch her, and his hand shook.

Xander placed a hand on Marina's shoulder and gave her a squeeze. "There are more just like her. Pregnant women, women with babies. Children, lots of them." He glanced at the trio of girls and gave them, what he hoped was, an encouraging smile. "It's going to be okay. We've got the answer right here."

Gavin's mouth opened and closed, then opened and closed again. Finally, a single, strangled word emerged. "How?"

At that exact moment, Cara arrived, along with six other pregnant women, and more than a dozen children of various ages.

Blinking at the sight, Gavin let his hand drop to his side and stumbled back a step.

Sabine dashed forward, gathering a sobbing Aria and her sisters into her arms. "It's okay, I'm here—I'm here. You did good."

"All this time…" Gavin approached the group of women and children who'd gathered behind Xander, his voice filled with awe. "I was wrong, so wrong. I didn't need to—" His gaze shot to the three girls, then Sabine. "I thought…it doesn't matter what I thought."

Xander held a hand up as Gavin got within arms-length.

"I'm not going to hurt them. I'm just… I want…"

A lengthy pause ensued until Sabine spoke. "Does this mean you'll help me? Do this my way?"

Without even looking at her, Gavin nodded, his attention fixated on the pregnant women.

Relieved, Xander met Dalton's gaze across the yard, and indicated the hut with the tip of his head. "Bring them out."

Dalton's eyes widened as a look of surprise crossed his face. "You sure?"

"Who, Xander?" Sabine asked, her gaze going to the hut. "Who's in there?"

"Do it," Xander said, certain this was his ace-in-the-hole. Once Gavin saw all his girls, saw them next to the healthy, pregnant women, the other children, the last of his doubts would be gone. He was sure of it.

Dalton went to the door and opened it.

One by one, beginning with Zuri, the albino second-gen clones shuffled out.

Gavin gasped.

Xander smiled…until Gavin turned on him, rage in his eyes.

"Kill them," Gavin bellowed. "Xander, Dalton, Sabine—kill them all."

The guards opened fire.

Twenty

As shots rang out, Sabine snatched Neriah up into her arms, then shoved Felicity and Aria toward the truck bed trailer. "Run!"

Once they were safe, she peeked out in time to see Xander hit the ground, blood pouring from wounds in his shoulder, leg, and side.

Screams filled the air. Girls ran everywhere, their striking white hair almost glowing amongst the other bodies racing for cover.

Trying not to draw attention to herself, she snagged a few of the girls as they ran by.

Across the yard, she saw Marina kneel by Xander, pressing her bare hands against his shoulder, when suddenly the woman's body jerked, and she fell backwards.

Albino girls and children from the hidden cavern swarmed Marina and Xander, and a few of their little bodies collapsed on top of them.

They're shooting kids! Bastards!

Sabine jumped up, waving her arms and yelling at the top of her lungs. "Stop!" She ran into the fray, ducking as a guard turned a gun toward her. Changing direction, she tackled Gavin. "They're killing your girls! Do something!"

Throwing her off, Gavin scrambled to his feet. "Cease fire!" he bellowed.

One by one, the guards stopped shooting.

But it was too late—far too late.

Sabine pounded a fist into the dirt as she began counting heads in the pile of bodies atop Xander and Marina. Tears streaming, she quit counting when she reached double digits. "You!" She launched herself at Gavin. "You did this!"

One of the guards caught her with an arm around the middle and flung her back to the ground. He pointed his gun at her and growled, "Stay down, if you know what's good for you."

Gavin sat in the dirt, face pale, mouth agape as he took in the scene.

Rounding up the surviving women and children, Dalton ushered them into the hut, muttering curses with every glance at the carnage.

Sabine was sat sobbing when a loud *clang* sounded from nearby. Whipping around, she froze at the sight before her.

R3...stumbling toward them, one hand clutching her largely swollen belly, while the other grasped the side of the trailer for support. Bright red blood from between her legs stained her gray overalls. She stretched a hand out to Gavin. "Help...me..."

The yard went deathly quiet, no sound except R3's panting and whispered pleas for help.

When Gavin didn't move, Sabine scrambled to her feet and hurried to the girl. She put an arm around her shoulders and steered her toward Dalton's hut. When she saw the place was near bursting with women and children, though, she changed direction, moving toward the barn instead.

"Someone, help us!" Sabine shouted.

No one moved.

R3's leg buckled, and she partially collapsed against Sabine.

"No, no, no..." Sabine hefted the girl up. "We're almost there." Her gaze flew around the yard, searching for help.

Dalton had all five guards standing with their hands on their heads and was pointing a gun at them. Two pregnant women were blocking the door to the hut. And

Gavin, he still sat on the ground, gaze glued to R3 as he rocked back and forth.

There was no help.

"C'mon," she said, tightening her hold on the girl. "Just a little further."

R3 took one more step, then went down in a heap, taking Sabine with her.

The girl was rank with the coppery scent of blood. Gasping and crying, she mumbled incoherent words as she grabbed at her belly.

Blood spread on the ground, soaking into Sabine's pant legs as she knelt beside the girl.

A tremor shook R3's tortured body, becoming a full-fledged seizure after a few seconds.

Helpless to do anything, Sabine rolled the girl to her side and waited.

When the shaking stopped, she turned her back over.

R3 was utterly still.

Sabine's heart hammered against her ribs as she felt for a pulse.

Nothing.

She laid her ear against R3's chest, listening.

Nothing. Not a damn thing.

It was the same as with the other two first gen models. When the programming terminated, it killed the unborn child too.

Sobs wracked Sabine's body.

R3 was dead, along with her baby.

Behind Sabine, a shuffling in the dirt. She glanced over her shoulder in time to see Gavin retrieve his gun from the ground.

He took two hesitant steps toward R3, then put the gun to his own temple. "I'm sorry, Rachelle," he said in a broken whisper.

"No!" Sabine screamed, reaching for him.

Gavin pulled the trigger, the side of his head exploding in a shower of blood and gore.

"Xander, can you hear me?"

It'd been two days since the massacre and he was still out. Sabine sat on a stool next to his cot at her place and poured more lake water over his wounds. She'd rigged an IV using materials from her make-shift clinic and had given some lake water that way, too.

She peeled back the pad on his shoulder, pleased to see the progress. He was healing, it was just taking some time. When the colonists had helped dig him out from under the pile of bodies, he'd been barely breathing.

Marina hadn't made it, neither had her baby. They'd lost a total of fourteen children, five of them second-gens. With no word from Trevor, and no way of knowing the state of things at RaShell, they'd sent the rest of the children, including the surviving clones, with the pregnant women back to the settlement deep within the cave and were being guarded around the clock now.

Beside her, Xander moaned.

"Hey…" She leaned over him, smiling when he opened his eyes. "There you are."

"Water," he croaked.

Grabbing a cup from a nearby table, she held it to his lips. "Slowly…that's right…"

After draining the cup, he relaxed against the straw-stuffed pillow. "What happened?"

She sighed and looked away, but the touch of his hand on her arm brought her back.

"Tell me."

"Gavin," she said, by way of explanation. "He found us, he…did this to you."

"What else?"

Teary-eyed, she relayed the rest of the story. "We buried the second-gens with R3," she finished. "I think she'd have liked that."

"Aria? Felicity? Neriah?" His voice cracked on the last name.

"They're safe. As soon as you're up and moving around, you can see them." She bit her lip, hesitant to give him the rest of her news, but there was no sense delaying it. "Xander?"

His eyebrows furrowed. "Yeah?"

"I'm going back to RaShell."

He frowned at her. "What? Why?"

"I have to. The world…it's still wrecked." She gave a vague gesture above her, toward the world outside of the cave. "I need to try and fix it. With the technology there, I just might stand a chance."

Reaching for her hand, Xander squeezed it. "I understand. Will you be back?"

"As soon as I can," she said, squeezing his hand in return.

ﻝ ﻝ ﻝ

A week later, Sabine arrived at RaShell, surprised to find everything looking much as it had before. As she approached, she saw workers in the greenhouses, and a guard greeted her at the gate.

"Sabine Reed," she said, reaching to remove her pack for her old ID.

The guard held up a hand. "I know who you are." He opened the gate and let her in. "We thought you might come back."

"We?" she asked, hesitantly stepping inside. The last thing she wanted was to be locked in that cell again.

"Gavin left Liliam in charge while he was gone," he replied, gesturing for her to go ahead of him. "She's in the nursery."

She followed the guard through the pristine white

hallways, through four sets of locked doors with more security measures than before, and finally into the nursery.

"Ma'am," the guard said, announcing their arrival.

Liliam looked up from where she was cuddling an adorable toddler with the trademark white hair. The child could have been Liliam's, the resemblance was so strong. Not surprisingly. After all, Gavin had used his and Liliam's DNA to provide the genetic material to copy for the second-gen clones.

Still, it was a bit unnerving when Liliam brushed her own shock white hair over her shoulder and studied Sabine with pale, icy eyes.

"Where's my husband?" she asked at last. "And don't beat around the bush about it. Just tell me straight."

"He's dead," Sabine admitted.

Liliam clenched her jaw, then visibly relaxed it. "Why are you here?"

Hoping to set the woman at ease, Sabine said bluntly, "To save the world, ma'am."

She gave a short, sharp laugh and shook her head. "God, you sound just like him."

Sabine wanted to assure her nothing could be further from the truth, but decided the wisest course of action was silence.

Liliam glanced over Sabine's shoulder to speak to

the guard by the door. "Brady, be a dear and bring me my medication, please."

"Right away, ma'am."

Liliam set the toddler down and gave her some toys, then motioned for Sabine to step to a window running the length of the room. On the other side were at least two dozen children, all appearing to be toddler aged. They watched them play for a few moments and Sabine noted the presence of an ample number of nurses as well as guards watching over them.

"That's all that's left of them," Liliam remarked as Brady returned with a syringe and an alcohol wipe. Her tone was nonchalant as she turned to Sabine with the needle in hand. "You stole the rest of my children."

Liliam stabbed Sabine in the neck and pressed the plunger before she could lodge a protest, or even move out of the way.

Within seconds, a wave of lightheadedness washed over her. "What was that?"

"Never you mind," Liliam said, patting her on the shoulder. She guided her to a rocking chair in the corner and helped her sit. "It'll all be over in a minute."

"But…why…" Sabine's tongue felt thick, and her words came out slurred.

"I couldn't protect Rachelle, dear, but these children? They'll never be harmed." She tucked a blanket around Sabine's legs, then went and picked up the little girl who was playing contentedly in the corner. "Come along, Mable, let's go see your sisters."

ﭲ ﭲ ﭲ

Days turned into weeks, then months with no word from Sabine, when Xander was summoned to Dalton's. "What's up?" he asked, stepping inside.

"Communication has finally been reestablished and I have a message." Dalton gestured to the empty chair at the table. "Might as well take a seat."

Anxiety tightened his stomach. It couldn't be good news if he needed to sit, but he did it anyway. "What've you heard?"

"Trevor and his team are all dead."

"And Sabine?"

"Missing." Dalton scrubbed a hand across his face. "She made it to RaShell and hasn't been seen since. That's all I know."

Xander slapped a hand on the tabletop. "Well, I better go—"

A knock sounded, then Aria poked her head in. "Xander, can I talk to you?"

"Sure kiddo, come on in."

As she entered the hut, he noticed her cheeks were flushed. "What is it? What's wrong?"

She closed the door and leaned against it, looking hesitant. "I, uh... I wish Sabine was here. Would be easier to talk to her."

Thinking to reassure her, Xander said, "I was just saying I should go look for her."

Aria's lips tightened and her eyes filled to the brim with tears, a few spilling over as she wiped her cheeks with a shaky hand.

"Aria, what's wrong?" Xander got up and stooped down in front of her. "Whatever it is, you can tell me."

"You can't go," she cried. "Promise you won't go. You can't leave me, you just can't."

He smoothed her hair back. "Hey, hey, slow down. What's going on?"

"My embryo…it triggered."

Xander rocked back on his heels. *Oh shit!* "You're…pregnant."

jodi jensen

Jodi Jensen

J odi Jensen is a multi-genre author who writes everything from Time-Travel Romance, to Sci-Fi, Horror, Paranormal, and now Biopunk.

On her lighter side, she has two time-travel romance novels published with Champagne Book Group, and on her darker side, nearly eighty short stories published with Black Hare Press, Black Ink Fiction, Fedowar Press, and Iron Faerie Publishing. She was the lead author on a collaborative horror anthology and has also self-published a children's book written for her autistic grandson.

Jodi is never afraid to try writing something new and

writes about whatever strikes her as inspirational, though she has a particular fondness for penning end-of-the-world stories.

Bibliography:

Children's Fiction
Luna Kitty in the Garden, Self-Published, 2021

Novels
Sophie's Key, Champagne Book Group, 2020
The Matchmaker's Charm, Champagne Book Group, 2022

Anthologies
13 Drops of Blood (Lead Author), Black Hare Press, 2021
Ancients (Dark Drabbles), Black Hare Press, 2020
Angels (Dark Drabbles), Black Hare Press, 2019
Apocalypse (Dark Drabbles), Black Hare Press, 2019
Avenge (Five Hundred Fiction), Black Hare Press, 2021
Bad Romance, Black Hare Press, 2020
Beyond (Dark Drabbles), Black Hare Press, 2019
Bloodlust (Legends of the Night) , Black Ink Fiction, 2021
Bones (Five Hundred Fiction), Black Hare Press, 2021
Contact (Five Hundred Fiction), Black Hare Press, 2021

Ctrl Alt Del (Revelations), Black Ink Fiction, 2021

Dragons (Five Hundred Fiction), Black Hare Press, 2023

Emerald City, Iron Faerie Publishing, 2021

Envy (Seven Deadly Sins), Black Hare Press, 2020

Gluttony (Seven Deadly Sins), Black Hare Press, 2021

Greed (Seven Deadly Sins), Black Hare Press, 2020

Hate (Dark Drabbles), Black Hare Press, 2020

Haunt (Five Hundred Fiction), Black Hare Press, 2021

Hell (Five Hundred Fiction), Black Hare Press, 2022

Infection (Legends of the Night) , Black Ink Fiction, 2021

Legends of the Night - A Horror Anthology, Black Ink Fiction, 2021

Lockdown Horror #1, Black Hare Press, 2020

Lockdown Phantom #1, Black Hare Press, 2020

Lockdown Sci-Fi #2, Black Hare Press, 2020

Love (Dark Drabbles), Black Hare Press, 2020

Lust (Seven Deadly Sins), Black Hare Press, 2020

Monsters (Dark Drabbles), Black Hare Press, 2019

Oceans (Dark Drabbles), Black Hare Press, 2020

Pestilence (Revelations), Black Ink Fiction, 2021

Play (Five Hundred Fiction), Black Hare Press, 2021

Pride (Seven Deadly Sins), Black Hare Press, 2020

Quietus 13, Black Hare Press, 2020

Reaperman (Legends of the Night), Black Ink Fiction, 2021

Reign (Five Hundred Fiction), Black Hare Press, 2021

Revelations, Black Ink Fiction, 2021

Sloth (Seven Deadly Sins), Black Hare Press, 2020

Tick Tock (Five Hundred Fiction), Black Hare Press, 2020

Unravel (Dark Drabbles), Black Hare Press, 2019

War, Black Hare Press,2022

Watch (Five Hundred Fiction), Black Hare Press, 2021

Weird Western Anthology, Bounties, Beasts and Badlands, Fedowar Press,2021

West (Five Hundred Fiction), Black Hare Press, 2023

Worlds (Dark Drabbles), Black Hare Press, 2019

Wrath (Seven Deadly Sins), Black Hare Press,2021

Connect:

Website: jodijensenwrites.wordpress.com/

Twitter: twitter.com/WritesJodi

Facebook: www.facebook.com/jodijensenwrites

Macabre Minima

Macabre Minima is a small, independent publisher based in Melbourne, Australia. Founded in 2018, our aim has always been to champion emerging authors from all around the globe and offer opportunities for them to participate in speculative fiction and horror short story anthologies.